CAPE MAY DREAMS

CLAUDIA VANCE

CHAPTER ONE

Margaret stared out the truck window as Dave drove down Long Beach Boulevard. Even in early October, it felt like August. It was an eighty-degree day, and it seemed every street corner had people waiting to cross while holding beach chairs and bags. "It's been a few years since I've been to Long Beach Island," Margaret said as a smile grew on her face. "I forgot how much I love it here."

"Same," Dave said as he switched off the air conditioner and rolled down his window. "I remember coming here as a teenager. I had friends whose parents rented a beach house in Beach Haven. They would get the house for a couple weeks, and I got to tag along. Had some great memories."

Margaret turned to Dave and cocked her head. "Really? I also came down with a friend's family during my teenage years. Their house was in Beach Haven too. I'm surprised this never came up in conversation with us."

Dave shrugged. "Yeah, that is strange. Guess we kind of forgot about it all these years."

Margaret nodded then stared out the window. "Probably. It is easy to get wrapped up in Cape May and the surrounding areas."

Dave glanced at the clock. "We still have a few more hours until check-in at the hotel. What should we do?"

Margaret looked at her phone. "Well, Liz and Greg are running late. Sarah and Chris are off somewhere around here with her cousins, and Donna and Dale will be getting here at five. Oh yeah, Nick and Lisa couldn't make it."

Dave turned the car into a shopping center parking lot. "Why don't we head to those tide pools I read about near the Barnegat Lighthouse? It's low tide, so we might catch them still."

"That could be fun," Margaret said as Dave pulled back onto the boulevard heading in the opposite direction.

They drove to the other end of the island until they got to the lighthouse. They each stepped out of the truck and took a deep breath of the salty air. Dave took Margaret's hand. "Let's follow the signs."

Out on the beach, they saw a walkway along the jetty by the water, and to the right of that were tons of tide pools, some with people walking around in them.

"There they are," Margaret said, pointing.

As they approached the tide pools, they took off their shoes and stood ankle-deep in the water, staring down at the sunlight's reflection. The water was warm, and there were some rocks and pieces of seaweed throughout. Up on the jetty in front of them were fishermen who were relaxing and chatting on the beautiful day.

"I like it here," Dave said as he turned his face to the sun and closed his eyes. "If we lived closer, I'd come more often."

Margaret smiled as she looked over to see some kids running toward a tide pool with their parents. "I like it here, too, but I was thinking we could get something to eat. I know we have dinner plans with the group later, but I'm starving," she said as she put her hand on her stomach.

Dave laughed. "I'm glad you said something. I was afraid

to mention it in case we ruined our appetites. Let's head back and go find something light to eat."

They were back on the road, and Margaret leaned her arm out the window as the light breeze ran through her hair. She watched as a large group of surfers on bikes holding their boards crossed in front of them. "There's a lot of surfers here. More so than I ever see near us."

Dave nodded in agreement as he spotted a sign up ahead. "The Local Market and Kitchen. Shall we try it?"

Margaret widened her eyes. "It looks perfect. They even have a nice outdoor seating area."

They parked and walked inside to an adorable but cool market with a deli, a baked goods area, and a place to order coffees, lattes, and more.

Margaret took in the bustling market, feeling overwhelmed by the many delectable choices. Then she watched as someone walked by with a scrumptious-looking sandwich. "That's what I'm getting."

After finding some cold drinks in the refrigerated case, they ordered their sandwiches then stood back and observed as they waited for them to be done. A couple came in with their new baby, grabbing goodies for the day ahead, then a gaggle of high school girls giggled as they waited in line to order s'mores lattes. Minutes later, some men with half-zipped wetsuits came in to order lunch after probably a long morning of surfing and working up an appetite.

Finally, Margaret's and Dave's orders were ready, and they headed outside, taking a seat at a shaded table. Dave took a sip from his bottle of sparkling water as Margaret unwrapped her bacon, lettuce, and fried green tomato sandwich.

"I should have gotten that. It looks amazing," Dave said as he started unwrapping his French ham baguette.

Margaret shook her head and laughed. "How about we each give each other half of the other's sandwich, because yours looks incredible. It reminds me of when I ate them almost every day in Paris."

"Deal," Dave said with a smile as they traded halves. Then they each took a bite and groaned.

Margaret glanced around her at all the other people near them eating, drinking, and conversing on the gorgeous day as soft reggae played on the outdoor speakers. "You know, it's amazing how each New Jersey beach town feels different from the others. I have to say LBI has a Southern California feel. It's very laid back and chill."

"Totally agree," Dave said then took a bite and swallowed. "There's Cape May with its historic Victorian homes and abundant wildlife and trails, then you have Avalon, Stone Harbor, Ocean City, Atlantic City, Strathmere, Sea Isle City, plus all these other shore towns even up north that I haven't gotten to yet. It's incredible, really. It makes you appreciate each place for what they have to offer and the feeling you get when you're there. I feel lucky to live here, even if we don't have gorgeous Hawaiian-style beaches. New Jersey beaches and coastal towns all have their own individualized beauty."

Margaret smiled. "You just said everything I wanted to say. Couldn't have said it better, really."

Dave glanced at his watch, noticing both he and Margaret were finished eating. "Looks like we can start heading to the hotel. By the way, whose idea was this? I'm kind of loving that this LBI weekend was organized. We should do this more often."

Margaret stood up, grabbing her trash and Dave's, then put it in the garbage can across from them. "I think it was Chris and Sarah's idea. I was kind of shocked when they brought it up because they've never really put together something like this before. Plus, I know they invited family, as their cousins are here with them. I don't know much about the plans, though. I guess we'll find out. Either way, I'm glad they rounded everyone up. It's going to be a fun weekend, and we'll be home in time to pick up the girls from my parents'."

"Perfect. Great timing, especially with having this nice relaxing weekend before we start remodeling the new beach house we just closed on. It's going to be a lot of work but gratifying work, that's for sure," Dave said as he put his arm around Margaret's shoulders, and they happily walked back to the truck.

* * *

After relaxing and freshening up at the hotel, Margaret and Dave met with the group at The Gables, a gorgeous restaurant in Beach Haven with the most exquisite menu.

Margaret wore a red knee-length dress with black strappy heels, and Dave had on khakis, a short-sleeve button-up shirt, and loafers.

"It's been some months since we've dressed up, no?" Margaret said to Dave as they walked down the sidewalk toward the restaurant.

"It has indeed," Dave said as he placed his hand on the small of Margaret's back.

"The last time I was here was years ago in June when the hydrangeas were blooming in front of the restaurant. There were explosions of purple flowers everywhere, and they had giant ferns hanging off the front porch. Not to mention the food. It was some of the best I've had," Margaret said as they walked into the restaurant.

"Table for two?" the host asked cheerily.

Margaret swept her gaze across the restaurant. "No, we're with a reservation under…"

Just then, Margaret heard her name being called.

She turned to see Liz, Greg, Donna, and Dale sitting on the front porch at a large table with candles lit.

Dave chuckled. "I think we found our friends," he said, leading Margaret to the table.

Everyone got up to give their hugs and hellos, and Margaret and Dave took the seats on the end next to Liz and Greg.

"This place is magical. I'm so glad Sarah and Chris chose here for a dinner meet up. By the way, where is Sarah and Chris?" Margaret asked as she peered through the crowded restaurant.

Donna chimed in, "They're on their way. I just got a text from them. Would you like some white or red wine in the meantime?" she asked while holding a bottle of red.

"Oh, wonderful. I'll have red please." Margaret glanced at Dave. "What are you feeling tonight?"

Dave chuckled. "I guess red, it is."

Just then, the sun fully set, and the candles on the table glowed even brighter as the sky grew completely dark.

Liz nudged Margaret under the table then whispered into her ear, "I think something is up."

"What do you mean?" Margaret asked as she took a sip from her wineglass.

Liz shrugged. "I don't know. I'm getting weird vibes."

Margaret furrowed her brow. "From who?"

Before Liz could answer, Chris and Sarah came up behind her and Greg, holding two bottles of wine, and placed them on the table.

"Bet you thought we'd never make it," Chris said with a hearty laugh.

"Finally!" Margaret said, laughing, as she and Dave got up to greet them with the rest of the table.

"We're only thirty minutes late," Sarah said as she pointed at Chris's foot. "We spent the entire day at the emergency room."

"What?" Dale asked as he glanced down. "What happened to your foot, man?"

Chris glanced at the black walking boot he was wearing. "I severely sprained it today while walking down the steps to the beach. Missed a step and rolled my foot good. When I tell you the pain I had from this was on another level. I think people on the other side of the island heard my screams. I was almost positive I broke it. It took six hours at the local ER to get seen, get X-rays, and get a diagnosis and treatment. Thankfully, it's not broken," he said while taking a seat.

Greg shook his head. "I've never sprained my foot, but I have rolled my ankle a handful of times throughout life. It's some of the worst pain. Sorry, man. I hope the swelling and pain go down soon."

"Where are your cousins that you were with today?" Margaret asked Sarah as she sat down next to Dave.

Sarah shook her head solemnly. "Sick with food poisoning or a stomach virus. They aren't sure what, but they can't even keep water down. They're in the hotel room."

"My gosh!" Liz said as she held her hand over her mouth.

Sarah sighed. "Oh, I know. This wonderful weekend is turning out to be anything but wonderful for us. Hopefully, you all are enjoying yourselves, though," she said with a forced smile, glancing around the table.

Everyone was too nervous to do much but nod and smile at Sarah as they sheepishly took sips of their wine.

Ten minutes later, they had ordered their food and were all conversing when Chris grew quiet. He sat back in his seat, deep in thought, then interrupted everyone.

"Well, look. Here's the real reason we put together this weekend. It's not happening now, so we might as well come out with it," Chris said as he glanced at Sarah.

Sarah shook her head at him. "No, we'll tell them another time."

Everyone at the table sat there in silence, staring at them, now wanting to know *why* they were there.

Chris sighed deeply and sat back in his chair and folded his arms.

"Fine. You can tell them," Sarah said.

Chris blurted it out almost immediately. "We were trying to do a surprise wedding this weekend, similar to how Dave and Margaret had theirs," he said glancing at Margaret and Dave. "But between my foot ordeal, her cousins getting sick—who, by the way, one of them was going to marry us—and multiple close family members that now can't make it tomorrow, including Sam, who has a rescheduled soccer game, we're not following through with it."

Sarah looked defeated. "It's fine. This was kind of a last-minute decision, and Chris wasn't totally on board with it. It was mainly my idea, but now I'm seeing that I wasn't being totally considerate of Chris's feelings."

Chris put his arm around Sarah. "I would've been fine with it had it worked out better. Having our family at the wedding is important, and if they don't know we're having a surprise wedding, then it might be hard to get them here, you know?"

Just then, the lights flickered, and the air got a little colder. Margret put her cardigan on and scooted her chair closer to Dave for warmth. "I think you two will find the perfect way to have a wedding even if this didn't work out. I'm excited for that day."

"Hear! Hear!" everyone at the table said, holding up their wineglasses for a cheers.

Chris and Sarah kissed then held up their wineglasses just as their food arrived at the table.

A half hour into dining, the lights flickered again, and a cold wind gust came in.

Chris looked at his phone. "We're due for a bad storm pretty soon, it looks like. Shall we finish up? We rented a little one-bedroom beach house for the weekend if you'd like to come by and hang out for the rest of the evening."

"Sounds great," Donna said then finished her last bite.

* * *

Twenty minutes later, they were all conversing and laughing in the living room of Chris and Sarah's beach house in Beach Haven.

"This might be the house that my friend's family rented when I was kid," Dave said, taking in the surroundings.

"Really?" Margaret asked.

Dave shrugged. "Maybe not. I guess a one-bedroom wouldn't have worked with all of their kids plus me," he said with a chuckle.

Sarah brought out some beers and wine for everyone and threw down a deck of Uno cards. "Who's in?" she asked.

Liz stood up abruptly. "Oh, you know I'm in."

Margaret rolled her eyes. "You don't want to play Uno with Liz. She gets so competitive. It gets nasty. Trust me. I was her main playing partner for years."

Chris laughed. "Even better!"

Margaret glanced at Dave and laughed. "I can't believe I'm willingly playing this with her."

Liz sighed as she shook her head at Margaret. "You've got to give it up, sis. You only hate playing because I always win."

Suddenly, a crack of thunder boomed outside, out of nowhere, causing everyone to jump and scream just as howling winds picked up.

"Guys, I think the storm is officially here," Dave said as he got up to look out the window, now seeing sheets of rain coming down.

Sarah stood next to Dave, watching the winds and rain. "I think this surprise wedding was definitely not meant to be. I mean, look at this. It would have been a muddy mess tomorrow. Okay, who's ready to play the game?" she asked, turning back around.

Then the lights flickered, and the power went completely out. Everyone sat in silence for a moment, then they all burst out into laughter over the irony of everything going wrong. Humor turned out to be the best medicine for wedding plans gone awry.

CHAPTER TWO

The weekend at Long Beach Island had been cut short. After a night of laughing through the power outage at Chris and Sarah's beach house, Margaret and Dave decided to leave early Sunday morning, as the power was still out, and they were able to cancel their second night at the hotel. They drove back to Cape May and headed straight to their new beach house, as Harper and Abby had a day at the zoo and an evening of games planned with Judy and Bob.

A couple of hours of driving later, they stood in front of their newest project: a charming but weathered wood-sided cottage they'd recently purchased. Located on a one-way alley just two blocks from the beach, the old Cape May home sat hidden under big, shady oak and maple trees.

The morning brought with it a gentle breeze carrying the scent of salty air, and Margaret took a deep breath as Dave jimmied the key into the front door's ancient lock.

"Ready to see what we've gotten ourselves into?" Dave asked with a mix of excitement and trepidation in his voice.

Margaret nodded, clutching her to-go coffee. "As ready as I'll ever be."

The door creaked open, revealing a space that echoed with

decades of memories. Dust particles danced in the sunlight that streamed through the windows, illuminating the worn hardwood floors and the kitchen, which looked like it hadn't been updated since the 1990s.

"I know the inspector said the foundation was solid, but everything else..." Dave ran his hand along the wall, feeling the uneven texture beneath his fingertips.

Margaret walked in and set her coffee down on the kitchen counter and pulled out her phone. "I've got my list right here. I don't even know where we should begin," she said then scanned the house. "We've got our work cut out for us. It sure looks more weathered without all of Howard's furniture and decorations in here."

Dave walked to the sliding glass doors that led to the screened-in porch and then to the large backyard beyond. Salt and time had corroded the tracks, making the door stubborn about opening. With a grunt and a forceful push, he managed to slide it open. "Add 'replace sliding doors' to that list."

As they spent the morning assessing the house, their to-do list grew longer by the minute. The plumbing needed a complete overhaul. The electrical system was outdated and potentially dangerous. The roof had several spots where it would need to be patched. Dave paused in the stairway, admiring the beautiful stained-glass window that cast colorful patterns on the wall as light streamed through it.

"This is definitely staying," he said, pointing at the window. "Howard, the previous owner, was right—it's gorgeous."

Margaret smiled, making a note in her phone. "Agreed. That's one of the vintage charms we need to preserve."

By lunchtime, they sat on the old rocking chairs on the screened-in porch, eating sandwiches from the cooler they'd packed.

"It's definitely going to be more work than we anticipated," Margaret said then took a bite of her turkey sandwich.

Dave nodded, his eyes taking in the lush backyard with its

tall trees and the shrubs that lined the fence. "But think of how amazing it's going to be when we're done. Our own little slice of paradise just a short walk from the beach. And that private path Howard showed me—that's worth its weight in gold."

Margaret smiled, leaning back in the rocking chair. "I still can't believe how close it is to the Seahorse Inn."

After lunch, they decided to divide and conquer. Dave would start tearing up the old, stained carpet in the living room, and Margaret would begin cataloging what they'd need for the bedrooms upstairs.

"I'll pick up those paint samples tomorrow," Dave called up the stairs as Margaret made her way to the second floor.

The wooden stairs groaned under her weight, and Margaret made a mental note to add "reinforce staircase" to their growing list. The upstairs hallway was narrow, with three small bedrooms and a bathroom that looked like it hadn't been updated since the 1970s, complete with avocado-green tile.

Margaret worked her way through each bedroom, measuring windows for new curtains and noting areas where the walls would need patching. In the smallest bedroom, she opened the closet door to find it empty except for a single wire hanger dangling from the rod.

As she was about to close the door, something on the top shelf caught her eye. It was a box pushed far back against the wall, almost invisible in the shadowy recesses of the closet. Margaret reached up, her fingers brushing against the dusty cardboard.

Standing on her tiptoes, she managed to grasp the edge of the box and carefully pull it forward. It was heavier than she'd expected, and as she brought it down, a cloud of dust erupted, causing her to sneeze.

"You okay up there?" Dave called from downstairs.

"Fine!" Margaret responded, waving away the dust. "Just found an old box in the closet."

She carried the box to the middle of the room, where the

light was better, and sat cross-legged on the floor. The box was a weathered shoebox, its cardboard soft with age. Carefully, she removed the lid to reveal a collection of envelopes yellowed with time and tied together with a faded blue ribbon.

Margaret gently untied the ribbon and picked up the top envelope. The handwriting was elegant, flowing script, addressed to "My dearest Eleanor." The return address indicated it was from someone named William Phillips, postmarked 1952.

Her heart quickened as she realized what she'd found—love letters, decades old, full of history and emotion. Carefully, she slid the letter from the envelope and began to read.

My dearest Eleanor,

The summer is almost upon us, and I count the days until I can return to Cape May, to our charming cottage down the shore, and most importantly, to you. The winter has been long and gray without your smile to brighten my days. I dream of our walks along the beach, of the way the sunset paints your hair with golden light, of the sound of your laughter mixing with the calls of the seagulls.

The business in Philadelphia keeps me busy, too busy for my liking, but I find solace in knowing that each day brings me closer to June, closer to you. I've begun making arrangements for some improvements to the house—a fresh coat of paint for the porch, new curtains for the front windows (the ones you admired in that catalog I showed you), and perhaps, if time permits, that garden bench we spoke of for the backyard shade.

Do you remember how we sat on the porch last summer, watching the stars reflect on the quiet street, making plans for a future that seemed both impossibly distant and tantalizingly close? I think of that night often, of the promise in your eyes when you spoke of the life we might build together.

Until June, I remain forever yours, William

Margaret's eyes welled with tears as she finished reading. She was so engrossed in the letter that she didn't hear Dave's footsteps on the stairs.

"Making progress?" Dave asked, appearing in the doorway.

Margaret looked up, blinking away tears. "Dave, you have to see what I found."

Dave crossed the room and knelt beside her, peering into the box. "What are these?"

"Love letters," Margaret said, carefully handing him the one she'd just read. "From someone named William to a woman named Eleanor. Dated 1952."

Dave read the letter, his expression softening. "Wow. This is... This is really something."

Margaret nodded, looking back at the box full of envelopes. "I wonder who they were. Did they end up together? Did they live in this house?"

"The letter mentions Cape May and 'our charming cottage down the shore,'" Dave said, rereading a passage. "It's got to be this place, right?"

Margaret carefully replaced the first letter in its envelope. "I think so. There must be dozens more in here. I can't wait to read through them."

Dave glanced at his watch and handed the letter back to Margaret. "I should probably get back downstairs and finish tearing up that carpet before we lose the daylight. You can tell me about the rest of them later."

Margaret smiled, grateful for the chance to explore this treasure on her own. "I'll just read a couple more and then come help you."

Dave kissed the top of her head before standing up. "Take your time. This is a pretty amazing find."

As Dave's footsteps faded down the stairs, Margaret turned her attention back to the box of letters. She ran her fingers over the yellowed envelopes, each one a piece of someone's heart committed to paper. She selected another at random, this one from 1953, and carefully opened it.

As she read through William's words—his descriptions of his business challenges in Philadelphia, his longing for Eleanor, his plans for their future—Margaret felt as though she were being granted access to something precious and private. There were references to shared jokes, to moments Margaret could only imagine, to dreams that might or might not have come to fruition.

She put the letter back and selected another, noticing that the dates seemed to follow a pattern—most were written during winter and spring months, suggesting that perhaps William and Eleanor were together during summers in Cape May. Was this their vacation home? Did they live elsewhere for most of the year?

Margaret was about to open a third letter when she heard a loud crash from downstairs, followed by Dave's muffled voice.

"Everything okay down there?" she called, reluctantly setting the box aside.

"Just knocked over a paint can!" Dave called back. "Empty, thankfully!"

Margaret smiled, knowing she should go help him with the work they'd planned for today. She carefully retied the ribbon around the stack of letters and placed them back in the box, but as she was about to return it to the closet shelf, she noticed something she had missed before—a small, leather-bound notebook tucked at the bottom of the box.

With gentle fingers, she lifted it out, opening to the first page. In the same elegant handwriting as the letters, the inside cover read Eleanor's Diary, 1952-1955.

Margaret's breath caught in her throat. Here, perhaps, were answers to what had happened to William and Eleanor after that final letter she'd seen. But the sound of Dave struggling with something heavy downstairs reminded her of her priorities for the day.

"I'll be back," she whispered to the diary, carefully placing it back in the box with the letters. She returned the box to its hiding place on the closet shelf, promising herself she would continue this discovery another time. For now, there was a house that needed their attention—a house that had already seen at least two love stories unfold within its walls and was now witnessing the continuation of a third.

Back downstairs, Margaret found Dave tearing up the old carpet in the living room, revealing hardwood floors underneath that were worn but salvageable.

"These floors are going to look amazing once we refinish them," she said, kneeling down to examine the wood.

Dave nodded, wiping sweat from his forehead. "That's what I was thinking. A little sanding, some stain, and they'll be as good as new."

They worked side by side for the next couple of hours, Margaret helping Dave remove the last of the carpet and tacks. When they were finished, they stood back to admire their progress.

"One room down, and more to go," Dave said with a chuckle.

Margaret was about to respond when she noticed water seeping from under the kitchen door. "Dave, look!"

They rushed into the kitchen to find water spraying from under the sink, already flooding the floor.

"What the—" Dave dropped to his knees, frantically searching for the source of the leak.

Margaret pointed at a pipe that was visibly cracked and gushing water. "There! The pipe just gave way!"

Dave reached under the sink and felt around until he found what he was looking for. With a grunt, he turned a valve, and the flow of water gradually stopped.

They stood in the middle of the kitchen, surrounded by puddles, looking at each other in dismay.

"Well," Margaret said finally, "I guess we know what our first priority is now."

Dave nodded, pushing his wet hair back from his forehead. "Yep. Complete plumbing overhaul ASAP."

Margaret grabbed a roll of paper towels they'd brought and began mopping up the water. "You know what this reminds me of? William mentioned something in one of his letters about always promising to fix leaky faucets but never getting around to it."

Dave chuckled, joining her in the cleanup. "Some things really don't change, do they? This old house has probably seen its fair share of plumbing disasters over the years."

"Hey," Dave said after they'd made some progress with the cleanup, "why don't I run to the hardware store and get some supplies? We might as well start on the plumbing today, since it's clearly not going to wait for our schedule."

Margaret nodded, wringing out a soaked towel into a bucket. "Good idea. I'll finish cleaning up here."

As Dave gathered his keys and headed out, Margaret stood in the middle of the kitchen, taking in the dated cabinets and the old appliances. Despite the setback, she felt a surge of determination. Howard and his wife, Pat, had raised their children here, creating memories that had lasted a lifetime. William and Eleanor had shared their love in these rooms. Now it was their turn to add their story to the house's history.

When Dave returned from the hardware store thirty minutes later, he found Margaret in the kitchen, having finished the cleanup and now making notes about cabinet measurements.

"Got everything we need to fix that pipe," he said, setting down his bags. "And I picked up some sandpaper to start on those cabinet doors you wanted to refinish."

Margaret smiled at him. "Perfect. I think we can salvage a lot of the original woodwork with a little love."

"Find anything else interesting in those letters?" Dave asked as he began unpacking his supplies.

Margaret shook her head, deciding to keep the diary discovery to herself for now. "I just read a couple more. I put them back for safekeeping—there's a lot to go through, and we have work to do."

As they settled into their respective tasks, Margaret couldn't stop thinking about the letters and diary waiting upstairs. What stories did they contain? What had happened to William and Eleanor? Had they lived out their lives in this house or moved on? The mystery of the previous occupants added a layer of intrigue to their renovation project, one that Margaret was eager to unravel—but at her own pace, in her own time.

For now, though, there were pipes to fix and rooms to restore. The secrets of the past would have to wait just a little longer.

CHAPTER THREE

Greg locked up Heirloom, his Cape May restaurant, and stood on the front porch, looking out toward the street. He paused for a moment before he abruptly took a seat at one of the tables on the porch then took his laptop out of his bag and opened it. He pulled up his bookkeeping for the summer, which he'd finished the day prior, and stared at it in disbelief.

His cell phone rang, and he picked it up. "Hey, Liz."

"Hey. Are you on your way home?" Liz asked as she walked around the garage full of dust from sanding a hutch.

"I was…" Greg stared at his computer screen.

"What's going on? Everything okay at Heirloom? It's not that new cook, is it? Was he not as good as he seemed?" Liz asked as she picked up a can of stain and placed it on a stool.

Greg snapped out of his thoughts. "No. No, he's great. I just don't know how much longer I'm going to be able to employ him. I just looked at my numbers for this summer. Profits are down thirty percent from last summer. Thirty percent. I knew we were a bit slower this year, but I didn't realize that it was this bad."

Liz moved the can of stain and slumped down onto the stool. "This stinks. Why do you think business died down?"

"Honestly? I think it's partly because we're a BYOB. As cheaper as it is to bring your own bottle of wine or beers, people love having a drink made for them. There's something about having an old-fashioned on the rocks or a draft beer over bottled beer when you're out to dinner. I think that's part of it," Greg said as he watched a group of people walk by, heading toward Donna's Restaurant. "It's probably why Dale's place is thriving. He happened to take over the liquor license from the restaurant that was there prior. He picked the right spot."

Liz racked her brain. "It's gotta be more than that. Plenty of BYOBs in Cape May do well."

Greg nodded. "That's true. It would take a lot more research on my end to figure out why the decrease in customers, but honestly, it's easy to get overworked in the food industry. It's long days and, a lot of times, a fast-paced and high-stress atmosphere. I've been getting pretty burnt out with it for over a year now but have just been pushing through almost as if I'm trying to prove something."

Liz stood up and stretched. "If you close, what options do you think are out there for you?"

Greg sighed. "I could open up a much smaller establishment. A place that requires fewer employees, fewer surfaces to clean, and fewer hours. You know, like a small cafe or something. Maybe I could pick one thing and just do that. Maybe open a small shop and the only thing I sell is piping-hot scones."

"That's a thought, but would you have the start-up costs for that? What about…you go into business with me?" Liz asked without much thought.

Greg shook his head. "With restoring furniture?"

Liz nodded. "Yes, we both could work from home. We could tackle double the number of pieces that I'm getting done alone."

Greg bit his lip. "I'm not too keen on putting all of our

eggs in one basket right now. Plus, restoring furniture is not something I enjoy like you do. I think at this point I need to find my own thing that makes me money but that I enjoy doing."

"I get it. We can brainstorm later. I'm sorry Heirloom isn't working out," Liz said with a frown. "I know how much of yourself you poured into that restaurant."

"Thank you. I appreciate it. It's such a good location in Cape May too. I think I'm going to take a walk around town to clear my mind and maybe get some ideas," Greg said as he shut his laptop and put it back into his bag. "I'll call you when I'm heading home," he said before saying goodbye and hanging up.

Greg walked off the porch and down onto the sidewalk, heading toward Donna's Restaurant on the corner. The windows were open for the nice weather, and he caught a glimpse of Dale standing by the bar. He waved at him.

"Hey, man. What's going on?" Dale asked as he approached Greg.

Greg shook his head. "Just went over bookkeeping from the summer. Looks like I need to make some big changes. Thought I'd get some thinking done on a walk."

"That's a bummer. So sales weren't so good this summer?" Dale asked, feeling concerned.

"Thirty percent less than last summer. Heirloom just isn't cutting it anymore. How'd you do here?" Greg asked.

"We made about the same as last summer. I was disappointed, as I was pushing to at least have ten percent more in sales, but I guess I'll take it. Can I help with anything?" Dale asked.

Greg moved over to let a couple walk by. "Not at the moment. I may need your input once I figure out my next move, though. Honestly, I'm disappointed, but at the same time, I'm not. I'm burnt out. I'm ready for a change. This seems like the universe telling me that time for change is now."

Dale sighed. "I get it. I've been there. I talked to Donna about possibly buying the place next door and expanding this restaurant, but she talked me out of it. Getting too big will mean even more hours on my part. I'm already working sixty-hour weeks, but that's my fault because I'm dragging my feet on hiring a new manager. It's just so hard to find qualified and reliable people these days, and I hate the hiring process. It can be so time consuming with interviews, calling references, and all of that."

Greg put his hand on Dale's shoulder. "Get the manager hired before you burn out like me. Trust me."

Dale nodded as he looked back toward the restaurant. "I will. I promise. I actually have a good prospect coming to meet me in an hour. He used to manage a friend's restaurant in Collingswood years ago, so I already have good references for him. He's moved down here recently. Cross your fingers."

"Will do. All right, I'm going to head out. I'll give you a call later," Greg said then crossed the street, heading toward more restaurants and shops.

He walked about fifty feet when he stopped to peer inside Chocolate Days, a husband-and-wife-run shop full of store-made and imported chocolates. It was a smaller store, and the husband and wife usually took turns working there with the occasional college employees working nights and weekends during the summer. Today, the husband and wife, Robby and June, were together. They both looked happy and cheerful, and when they saw Greg, Robby waved him inside.

"Greg! How's life?" Robby asked as upbeat music played over the speakers throughout the store.

Not wanting to get into the details again with someone, Greg smiled. "It's going pretty well. How about you guys? Business good?"

June nodded enthusiastically. "Better than ever. We're heading off to Italy for two weeks this weekend," June said as she reached into the glass case, pulled out a chocolate bar, then handed it to Greg. "Here. Try this. It's the new Dubai chocolate bar with pistachio cream. It's all the rage right now."

Greg took a bite and was blown away. "I've heard of this. It's incredible. By the way, congrats on going to Italy. Are you having employees run the shop for you?"

Robby waved his hand in the air. "Well, just Friday through Sunday. The other days, we'll be closed with a sign on the door. We did it last year when we went to Ireland. It worked out really well."

June chimed in, "We went to Ireland for a whole month last year. Have you been? It's wonderful. I wanted to go back this year, but Robby wanted to try somewhere new. So Italy, it is."

Greg went into a daze. He'd never been to Italy or Ireland, and here this small business with a way less stressful atmosphere than Heirloom provided them with enough sales to not only live off of but to go abroad for a month as well. Perhaps he'd been doing this business thing wrong all along.

"Greg, you there?" June asked with a chuckle. "Still thinking about that heavenly Dubai chocolate?"

Greg laughed. "Sorry, my mind has been all over the place today. I'm actually thinking about making a big change over at Heirloom. Honestly, more than a big change. Probably closing the restaurant altogether. Sales just aren't what they used to be, but coming to your shop and seeing how you run things and how you live while owning a small business has motivated and inspired me just now."

"Really? I'm glad to hear that. You know, we used to run a restaurant before Chocolate Days. Over in Stone Harbor. Ten years, we kept the place open, then one day, after weeks and weeks of running ourselves ragged, I said, 'We're making a change,' and we did," Robby said.

June nodded in agreement. "We did. We made that change and never looked back. It was the best decision."

Greg felt hope and excitement fill him, and suddenly, he

was feeling more motivated than ever to figure out his next plan.

* * *

The sound of sanding filled the kitchen of Dave and Margaret's beach house. Margaret moved the sandpaper in small circles over the cabinet door laid across two sawhorses, the wood grain slowly emerging from beneath years of built-up finish.

Dave appeared from under the sink, wiping his hands on a rag. "I think we're good to go, for the kitchen, at least. New pipes are in, and I checked everything twice. No more leaks."

Margaret paused her sanding to smile at him. "You make plumbing look easy."

"I try," Dave said with a chuckle. "How are the cabinets coming along?"

"Slow but steady. The wood underneath is actually in pretty good shape. Nothing a little sanding and refinishing can't handle," Margaret said, brushing sawdust from the surface she'd been working on.

Dave walked over to the living room entrance and leaned against the doorframe as he surveyed the space. "I've been thinking about adding some built-in bookshelves on either side of the fireplace. Maybe a new mantel, too, as the one that's there is uneven and worn. Something craftsman style to match the character of the house."

Margaret set down her sandpaper and joined him, imagining the potential. "That would look amazing. It would really enhance the whole space."

"And the floors..." Dave said, looking down at the worn hardwood that extended from the living room into the dining room, where they had previously ripped the carpet up.

"They definitely need work," Margaret agreed. "But there's something about them that tells a story, you know? All those scratches and worn spots—they're like a roadmap of the lives lived here."

Dave put his arm around her shoulders. "I know what you mean. These old houses have so much character. You can feel the history in every room."

Margaret leaned into him. "We'll refinish them but keep their character. No perfect, glossy finish. Something that acknowledges the history but gives us a fresh start."

* * *

A couple of hours later, Margaret put down her sandpaper and joined Dave in the living room.

"I think I'm going to take a break," she said.

"Good idea," Dave replied, wiping sweat from his forehead. "I'll keep working on those built-in shelves I was telling you about. I want to get the measurements right before I start cutting any wood."

Margaret headed out the back door and stepped outside. She walked the perimeter of the property, taking mental notes. The grass was overgrown, but beneath the neglect, she could see the bones of what had once been a lovely garden. There were remnants of flower beds along the fence line, now mostly overtaken by weeds, and a few struggling rose bushes that had somehow survived years of minimal care.

As she made her way toward the back of the yard, near the shrubs that concealed the hidden path to the beach, something caught her eye. Half-hidden beneath an overgrown hydrangea was a rusted wrought-iron garden bench. Its scrollwork was still visible through years of neglect, and Margaret could tell it had once been quite beautiful.

She brushed away some of the foliage to get a better look. The bench was old but probably not as old as William and Eleanor's time here—likely a later addition from Howard and Pat's era. Still, seeing it made Margaret's mind wander to

William and Eleanor. Had they sat together somewhere in this very garden, watching the stars as they made plans for their future? Had Eleanor tended to the gardens that had once flourished here?

Margaret's curiosity about the previous owners intensified. She went back inside, finding Dave carefully measuring the wall space around the fireplace.

"I think I'm going to head to Beach Plum Farm for lunch," she said. "I need a break from all this dust. Did you want to come?"

Dave looked up from his tape measure. "That sounds amazing, but I think I want to keep working on these measurements while I have the idea fresh in my head. I'll probably walk down the street and pick up a sandwich later," he said with a smile.

"That works." Margaret nodded then headed upstairs. She quickly washed the sawdust from her hands, grabbed her purse, and on impulse, retrieved the box of letters from the closet shelf. She tucked her notepad into her bag and headed back downstairs with the box under her arm.

"I'll be back in an hour or so," she called to Dave, who was now sketching shelf dimensions on a pad of paper.

"Enjoy. I'll see you when you get back," Dave said as he came over and kissed the top of Margaret's head.

Fifteen minutes later, Margaret had arrived at Beach Plum Farm and had settled at a shaded picnic table. The organic farm with its rustic charm was one of her favorite places to think. Among the tables were raised garden beds full of plants like artichokes, mint, tomatoes, onions, and more. She ordered an egg salad sandwich and an iced tea from the kitchen and opened the box, carefully pulling out half of the sandwich.

This time, she approached the letters more methodically, arranging them by date. The earliest was from 1952, and they continued through 1955, though there were noticeable gaps.

She started a fresh page in her notepad, jotting down what she knew so far:

William & Eleanor - William worked in Philadelphia - They spent summers in Cape May at the cottage

She picked up a letter from 1953 that she hadn't read before. As she unfolded the delicate paper, she noticed it was from Eleanor to William, not the other way around.

My beloved William,

Your last letter brought such joy to my heart. I count the days until June when I can close up this dreary apartment and return to our little haven by the sea. The winter seems especially long this year, perhaps because I know what awaits me in Cape May—not just the cottage but you.

The teaching position continues to challenge me. The children are bright but restless as spring approaches. I can hardly blame them when I myself stare out the window during lesson preparations, dreaming of salt air and warm breezes.

I've been collecting seeds and planning our garden. Mrs. Holloway at the flower shop suggested a new variety of roses that would thrive in the sandy soil near the fence. I've also been thinking about that space beneath the oak tree—too shaded for most flowers but perfect, perhaps, for a small bench where we could sit in the evenings.

There is so much I want to tell you, so much I want to share, but some things are better said in person than committed to paper. Until June, know that you are in my thoughts constantly.

With all my love, Eleanor

Margaret sat back, processing what she'd learned. Eleanor had been a teacher. They had lived apart during the winters, with Eleanor apparently staying somewhere else while William was in Philadelphia. And Eleanor had indeed gardened at the cottage and wanted a bench for the shady spot.

She was about to open another letter when a familiar voice called her name.

"Margaret? Is that you?"

Looking up, Margaret saw Sarah walking toward her, a plate with a colorful farm salad in her hand.

"Sarah! What a surprise," Margaret said, gesturing to the empty spot across from her. "Join me?"

Sarah set down her plate and took a seat. "We just got home from LBI, and I told Chris I wanted to go get lunch while he dealt with work stuff. What are you up to? Playing hooky from renovation work?" She nodded toward the box of letters.

Margaret smiled. "Taking a break. You won't believe what I found in the closet of our beach house." She briefly explained about the box of letters and her growing fascination with William and Eleanor's story.

"That's incredible," Sarah said, eyeing the yellowed envelopes with interest. "It's like uncovering a real-life romance novel."

"I know. I can't stop thinking about them," Margaret admitted. "But enough about my obsession. How are you doing? I've been meaning to call and check in after everything that happened in LBI."

Sarah shrugged. "I'm okay. Better than I was, actually."

"How's Chris's foot?"

"Healing. He's still in the boot but can put more weight on it now. The worst part is that he can't captain his birding boat, which is making him a bit grumpy," Sarah said, absently mixing her salad.

"And the wedding plans?" Margaret asked.

Sarah sighed. "The truth is the whole 'surprise wedding' thing was mostly my idea. Chris went along with it to make me happy, but he wasn't sold on it."

"What made you want to do it that way?" Margaret asked.

"I loved how spontaneous and romantic your wedding to Dave was. No stress, no year of planning, just... love." Sarah twisted a napkin in her hands. "But what I realized is that what worked for you and Dave doesn't necessarily work for us.

Margaret nodded her understanding. "So what happens now?"

"We talked—really talked—on the drive home. He doesn't want a big or fancy wedding, but he does want our families to be there. So we have some options we're stewing over. I'll keep you updated when we figure it out... So enough about me—tell me more about these mysterious former owners of your beach house. Are you planning to try to track them down?"

Margaret glanced down at the letters spread before her. "I'm not sure yet. Part of me wants to know everything about them, and part of me likes the mystery. I found a diary, too, but I haven't had the courage to read it yet."

"A diary?" Sarah's eyes widened. "Oh, you have to read it! That's even better than the letters."

"I know, I know. I just... What if it doesn't have a happy ending? What if something terrible happened to them? I'm kind of attached to them already," Margaret admitted.

Sarah took a bite of her salad and swallowed. "That's the risk with any good story. But don't you want to know?"

Margaret nodded slowly. "I do. I'll try to read more letters tonight after the girls go to sleep." She began gathering the letters, carefully keeping them in chronological order. "Speaking of which, I should probably head back. We still have mountains of work to do."

CHAPTER FOUR

Donna tugged her sweatshirt closer around her as the morning breeze swept across Cape May Point. She adjusted her baseball cap and squinted to see someone approaching.

"Name?" asked the young woman with curly dark hair pulled into a messy bun. A name tag reading Ella - Beach Cleanup Coordinator was pinned to her denim jacket.

"Donna Blaston," she replied, smiling. "I saw the flyer at the Chamber of Commerce meeting last week."

Ella nodded appreciatively. "We're glad to have you! Not enough locals volunteer for these things. Mostly, we get summer people trying to give back before they head home for the season." She handed Donna a pair of thick gloves, a trash grabber, and two large biodegradable bags. "Green bag is for regular trash. Blue is for recyclables. We'll weigh everything at the end."

Donna took the supplies and stepped aside as more volunteers arrived. She hadn't planned on participating in a beach cleanup today—or ever, really—but seeing the flyer had triggered something. After her years of living in Cape May, she realized she'd never done anything like this. The beaches were always "someone else's responsibility," usually the city's. But after that meeting where the environmental commission had shared alarming statistics about marine debris, she'd decided it was time to get involved.

"Donna! Is that you?"

She turned to see Jerry, a fellow business owner from the Wildwood boardwalk, walking over with his own set of cleanup gear. He ran a T-shirt shop just a few storefronts down from her funnel cake stand.

"I didn't expect to see you here," Jerry said with genuine surprise. "Thought Saturdays were your busiest days at the stand."

Donna shrugged. "We're cutting back on fall hours. We'll be closed for winter pretty soon. Besides, thought it was time I did something different. I figured I'd try something new."

"Well, I've been doing this every month for two years now. You'll be amazed, and not in a good way, at what we find out there," Jerry said as he looked out toward the ocean.

The group of volunteers gathered around Ella for instructions. There were about twenty people in total, a mix of ages and backgrounds—a few families with teenagers, several retired couples, and a handful of individuals like Donna.

"We'll be working the stretch from Cape May Point State Park beach to Sunset Beach today," Ella explained, pointing down the shoreline. "We'll break into teams of three or four. Try to stay within sight of the other groups. If you find something unusual or too large to handle, just flag me down, as I'll be moving between groups."

Ella quickly sorted them into teams, and Donna found herself grouped with Jerry, a college student named Aiden who was working on an environmental science project, and an older woman named Faye who had been doing beach cleanups for decades.

"I overheard this is your first beach cleanup. You're in for an education," Faye told Donna as they headed toward their assigned section of beach. "People have no idea what's really out here until they start looking."

Donna nodded, thinking that after years of beach walks, she'd seen it all. But within minutes of starting, she realized how wrong she'd been.

The first hour was eye-opening. What had looked like a relatively clean beach from a distance revealed its secrets up close—cigarette butts by the dozens; tiny plastic fragments in colors nature never intended; bottle caps, straws, food wrappers partially buried in the sand and fishing line tangled in seaweed. Each item went into her rapidly filling bags.

"I had no idea," Donna said, pausing to wipe her brow. "I mean, I know there's trash on the beach, but... this much? And we're not even in tourist season anymore."

Jerry nodded knowingly. "Most of it washes in with the tide. Some comes from offshore. Some from up the coast. The ocean connects us all, including our garbage."

As they worked farther down the beach, away from the more popular areas, the nature of what they found began to change. The human debris became less frequent and the natural treasures of the beach, more apparent.

"Oh my goodness, look at this," Donna called, carefully picking up a delicate dried seahorse about the size of her thumb. It was flawlessly preserved, its curled tail and distinct shape intact.

"Nice find," Aiden said, coming over to look. "It was probably carried in by the current after that recent storm."

Donna placed it carefully in her belt bag. She'd find a small jar for it later.

As the morning progressed, she discovered more natural wonders—dried starfish in various sizes, their arms intact despite their journey; sand dollars bleached white by the sun, some broken but many whole; even a translucent shell she'd seen many times before that Faye identified as a jingle shell. "The kind they used to make wind chimes from."

"I've walked these beaches for years," Donna said, shaking her head in wonder. "How have I never noticed all this before?"

"Most people don't look down," Faye replied simply. "They look at the horizon, at the waves, at their companions. But the beach has its own little museum if you just look at your feet."

By midday, they had filled multiple bags and had worked their way along the beach, heading in the direction of Sunset Beach. As they approached a section of protected dunes roped off from public access, Donna paused to look at her surroundings.

Jerry stopped abruptly, pointing toward the dunes ahead. At first, Donna couldn't understand what she was seeing. It looked like strange black growths emerging from the sand. Then as they got closer, she realized what they were.

"Tires?" she said incredulously. "In the dunes?"

It wasn't just a few. As they approached, they could see dozens—no, hundreds—of old tires partially buried in the sand dunes. Some were almost completely covered, suggesting they'd been there for some time. Others looked more recent.

"This is... This is unbelievable," Aiden said, pulling out his phone to take pictures. "This has to be illegal dumping."

Faye was already waving her arms to get Ella's attention. "We're going to need a much bigger crew," she muttered.

Ella jogged over, her expression changing from curiosity to shock as she saw what they'd discovered.

"I've been coordinating cleanups for three years, and I've never seen anything like this," she said, surveying the scene. "These weren't washed up. Someone drove them here and dumped them."

"But why?" Donna asked, still trying to process the scale of what they were looking at. "It would take multiple trips, multiple vehicles. Why go to all that trouble just to illegally dump tires on a beach?"

"Disposal fees," Jerry explained grimly. "Proper tire disposal is expensive, especially in these quantities. Some unscrupulous business decided to save money by dumping them here instead."

Ella was already on her phone, taking photos and making calls. The other volunteer groups had noticed the commotion and were making their way over, expressions of disbelief forming as they realized what had been discovered.

"The city can't handle this with just standard beach cleanup equipment," Ella said after finishing a call. "These are embedded in the dunes. We'll need heavy machinery, and we'll need to be careful not to damage the dune structure itself—it's critical for storm protection."

Donna looked at the black rubber mounds stretching across the dune area. "So what happens now?"

Ella sighed. "Now we document everything, report it to the proper authorities, and start figuring out how to mobilize a much larger cleanup effort. This is going to take coordination between the city, the environmental commission, and maybe even state resources."

Aiden was checking something on his phone. "Some of these tires look like they've been here for years. The older ones are starting to break down. That's really bad. Tire rubber contains all sorts of chemicals that leach into the environment."

Donna felt a surge of indignation rising within her. This was her beach, her community. She'd taken it for granted for too long, assuming someone else was taking care of it. Now she was face-to-face with evidence that sometimes, things fell through the cracks—big things that could harm the delicate coastal ecosystem she loved.

"We need to get the community involved," she said

suddenly. "Not just the usual environmental volunteers. We need businesses, schools, everyone."

Ella looked at her with interest. "You have something in mind?"

"I own a funnel cake shop on the Wildwood boardwalk," Donna explained. "We have connections with other boardwalk businesses, with tourists, with locals. We can help spread the word. Maybe organize fundraising if special equipment is needed. My husband, Dale, knows people who might have equipment that could help."

Jerry nodded approvingly. "That's the spirit, Donna. This is too big for just the regular beach cleanup crew."

As the group began documenting the tire dump and discussing immediate next steps, Donna felt a strange mix of emotions. She was horrified at the environmental damage, angry at whoever had so callously dumped their waste on this beautiful shore, but also oddly energized. For the first time in years, she felt like she was seeing her community with fresh eyes—both its vulnerability and its potential.

"I can't believe I never came to these cleanups before," she told Jerry as they headed back toward the lighthouse, leaving Ella and a few others to continue documenting the tire site. "I always thought I appreciated the beach, but I never really saw it until today."

Jerry smiled. "That's how it starts. One day, you're picking up trash. The next, you're leading the charge to solve bigger problems."

Donna glanced back at the distant dunes where they'd made their discovery. Her Saturday had taken an unexpected turn, but so had something inside her.

She pulled the dried seahorse from her belt bag and looked at it thoughtfully. Such a delicate creature yet strong enough in its design to survive the tumultuous ocean and wash ashore intact. There was a lesson in that, she thought.

"So will we see you at next month's cleanup?" Jerry asked.

Donna smiled, tucking the seahorse carefully away. "Next month? I think you'll be seeing me a lot sooner than that. We've got work to do."

* * *

"This is it?" Nick asked, frowning as he pulled his truck to a stop in front of the first house on their list.

Lisa consulted the printout she'd received from the Realtor. "According to these directions, this is the place."

They both stared through the windshield at what could generously be called a house. The small ranch-style building had faded yellow siding, several boards of which were hanging at awkward angles. One of the front windows was covered with plywood, and the concrete steps leading to the door were cracked down the middle, with weeds growing through the fissure.

"The listing said 'handyman special,'" Lisa remarked, trying to find something positive to say. "I guess that wasn't an exaggeration."

Nick took a deep breath and switched off the ignition. "Well, we're here. Might as well take a look."

They climbed out of the truck and approached the house cautiously, as if it might collapse at any moment. The smell of mildew hit them before they even reached the front door.

"The Realtor said she left it unlocked for us," Lisa said, reaching for the tarnished doorknob.

The door stuck, requiring Nick to put his shoulder against it and push. It finally gave way with a groan of protest from the hinges.

Inside was worse than outside. The carpet, which might once have been beige, was now a patchwork of stains in varying shades of brown and gray. Water damage spotted the ceiling, and the wallpaper in the small living room was peeling away in strips.

"Oh my God," Lisa whispered, covering her nose with her hand. "It smells like something died in here."

Nick ventured farther into the house, wincing as the floorboards creaked ominously beneath him. "This place would need to be gutted completely. Maybe even torn down to the foundation."

Lisa carefully stepped around a suspicious dark spot on the carpet to join him in what appeared to be the kitchen. One cabinet door hung by a single hinge, and the linoleum floor was curling up at the edges.

"The listing mentioned views of the marsh," she said, peering through a grimy window. "I guess that's true, at least."

Nick opened what he assumed was a pantry door, only to quickly slam it shut again when something small and furry scurried across the floor inside.

"Nope. That's it. We're done here," he declared, already heading toward the front door. "I don't care if they're giving this place away. It would cost a fortune to fix, and I don't think I'd ever get the smell out of my clothes."

Back in the truck, Lisa crossed the first address off their list with perhaps more vigor than necessary. "Well, that was educational," she said, trying to lighten the mood. "At least we know what the absolute bottom of the market looks like."

Nick laughed, the tension leaving his shoulders. "You're right. It can only go up from here, right?"

"Right," Lisa agreed, though neither of them sounded entirely convinced. "Next stop is closer to town. The Realtor said it's small but recently renovated."

Twenty minutes later, they pulled up in front of a much more promising-looking property. The house was indeed small—a compact two-story with blue siding and white trim. The yard was neatly kept, with a few rosebushes lining the short walkway to the front door.

"This is more like it," Nick said, his optimism returning as they approached the house.

This time, the Realtor had arranged to meet them. Caitlin Wilkins was waiting on the front step, scrolling through her phone. She looked up as they approached, her professional smile appearing instantly.

"You must be Nick and Lisa! So glad you could make it," she said, extending her hand. "I think you're going to love this one. It's got so much character!"

The phrase "so much character" turned out to be Realtor-speak for "awkward layout and strange design choices." The front door opened directly into a kitchen that was indeed newly renovated but with countertops of an alarming shade of orange.

"The previous owner was quite... artistic," Caitlin explained, gesturing toward the backsplash made of what appeared to be broken CDs. "They wanted something unique."

"They certainly achieved that," Lisa murmured, catching Nick's eye.

The main floor consisted of just the kitchen and a small living area with a ceiling so low that Nick had to duck slightly to avoid hitting his head on the light fixture.

"Perfect for entertaining," Caitlin said brightly, though it was clear that more than four people would make the space uncomfortably crowded.

The tour continued upstairs via a spiral staircase so narrow that they had to ascend single-file, with Nick's shoulders brushing both walls.

"Very... cozy," Nick commented, trying to be polite.

The upper floor contained two small bedrooms and a bathroom that had been renovated with the same flair as the kitchen. The shower stall was tiled in a mosaic depicting a large, somewhat menacing-looking octopus.

"The previous owner was very into marine life," Caitlin explained, as if that clarified why anyone would want to shower with an angry cephalopod staring at them.

The second bedroom had been converted into what Caitlin

described as a "meditation space," featuring floor-to-ceiling mirrors on all walls and a ceiling painted to resemble a night sky, complete with glow-in-the-dark stars.

"It's... something," Lisa said, struggling to find anything positive to say.

"The location is great," Caitlin continued, undeterred by their obvious lack of enthusiasm. "Just a ten-minute drive to downtown, and there's a nice little coffee shop just around the corner."

As they headed back downstairs, Nick's expression made it clear to Lisa that this house was also a no-go. The layout was too awkward, the design choices too bizarre, and the location a little too far from where he needed to be. Plus, he'd have to duck every time he walked through his own living room.

Back in the truck, with promises to Caitlin that they'd "think about it," Nick let out a long sigh.

"I'm starting to think I should just buy a tent and pitch it on the beach," he said, only half joking.

Lisa consulted their list again. "We have one more for today. The Realtor didn't have much information on it—just a description that says, 'Pending renovation, owner selling as-is.' It's out near the bay."

Nick furrowed his brow. "That's pretty isolated."

"Worth a look, though." Lisa suggested. "It's on our way back anyway."

Nick nodded, starting the truck. "Might as well complete the tour of disappointment."

They drove north along the coast, eventually turning onto a narrow road that wound through dense trees before opening up to reveal glimpses of the Delaware Bay. The farther they went, the more skeptical Nick became.

"Are you sure this is right?" he asked as the road narrowed even further, becoming little more than a sandy lane.

Lisa checked the GPS on her phone. "According to this, we're almost there."

Around the next bend, the trees opened up to reveal a small clearing, and there it was—a modest cottage perched right on the edge of the bay. The house was small but sturdy-looking, with weathered gray shingles and a deep porch that wrapped around two sides. Large windows faced the water, and a set of wooden steps led down to a small private beach.

They parked and approached slowly, both of them suddenly quiet. There was no Realtor here—just a lockbox on the door with the code Lisa had been given.

The interior was simple but charming. The front door opened into an open-concept living space with vaulted ceilings and exposed beams. A stone fireplace dominated one wall, while the opposite wall was mostly windows, framing a breathtaking view of the bay. The kitchen was small but functional, with solid-wood cabinets and a butcher-block island. A short hallway led to two bedrooms and a bathroom—all modest in size but well-proportioned.

What really sold the place, however, was the deck. Accessible through sliding doors from the living room, it stretched the entire length of the house, providing an unobstructed view of the water. A set of stairs at one end led directly to the beach.

"Wow," Nick said simply, leaning against the railing and looking out at the bay. The late-afternoon sun cast a golden glow over the water, and in the distance, they could see a few sailboats making their way toward the harbor.

Lisa joined him at the railing, their shoulders touching. "It's pretty amazing," she agreed.

"It needs work," Nick acknowledged, gesturing toward some peeling paint and a few loose boards on the deck. "But structurally, it seems solid. And this location..."

"It's perfect for you," Lisa said softly. "Close enough to town and your oyster farm but private. Peaceful."

They spent another hour exploring the property, finding new things to love with each discovery. There was a small shed that could store Nick's surfboards, and the property backed up to a protected nature preserve, ensuring that the surrounding area would remain undeveloped.

As the sun began to set, they sat side by side on the steps leading to the beach, watching the changing colors reflected on the water.

"I can see myself here," Nick said finally. "Mornings on the deck with coffee before heading to the farm. Evenings watching the sunset. It feels right."

Lisa smiled, bumping her shoulder against his. "It suits you. It's peaceful but not isolated, simple but full of character—the real kind, not the Realtor kind."

Nick laughed then grew serious again. "It's a big step, though. Another mortgage, more responsibility."

"But freedom," Lisa pointed out. "No more dodging your parents' clutter or hiding in your shed. Your own space, finally."

Nick nodded slowly, his mind clearly made up. "I'm going to make an offer. Tomorrow morning, first thing."

"Good," Lisa said. "It's ideal for you."

"For now," Nick replied, giving her a sidelong glance. "Who knows what the future holds, right?"

They sat in comfortable silence for a while longer, watching as the first stars appeared in the darkening sky. The gentle rhythm of waves lapping against the shore provided a soothing backdrop to their thoughts.

"So," Nick said eventually, "want to help me pick out furniture that isn't orange?"

Lisa laughed. "Absolutely. Though I have to say that octopus shower was really something."

"I think I'll pass on bringing tentacles into my bathroom, thanks," Nick replied with a grin.

As they reluctantly prepared to leave, Nick took one last look around, trying to commit every detail to memory. This place felt right in a way that nowhere else had in a long time—not just as a house but as a home. A place where he could imagine building a future, maybe even sharing it with someone special.

He glanced at Lisa, who was closing the sliding door to the deck, her profile silhouetted against the last light of day. She caught his eye and smiled, and Nick felt something settle inside him. Whatever came next, he was heading in the right direction.

CHAPTER FIVE

Bob stepped out of his Cape May home with no particular destination in mind. The October air carried just enough chill to warrant the light jacket he'd grabbed on his way out, but the sunshine promised a pleasant day ahead. Judy had gone to yet another bookstore, and Bob had a few hours to fill.

"I'll walk down to the beach," he muttered to himself, but his feet seemed to have other ideas. Instead of turning toward the ocean, he found himself wandering toward Rotary Park.

The park was quiet on this weekday morning. A couple of mothers pushed strollers along the path, and an elderly man walked his miniature schnauzer, who stopped to investigate every blade of grass. Bob ambled along, hands in his pockets, enjoying the solitude.

He was about to turn onto another path when something caught his eye. At a small folding table, a man sat alone, his attention focused on a chess board in front of him. The man, who appeared to be around Bob's age, sat perfectly still, studying the pieces as if waiting for them to move on their own.

Bob hadn't played chess in years—decades, maybe. His father had taught him when he was ten, and he'd played regularly in college, but marriage, kids, career, and life, really, had pushed the game to the periphery. Still, he felt a pull toward the table and the solitary player.

"Morning," Bob said as he approached.

The man looked up, a smile immediately transforming his weathered face. "Good morning! Care for a game?"

Bob hesitated. "I haven't played in a long time. I'd be pretty rusty."

"That's fine by me," the man replied, gesturing to the empty chair across from him. "It's not about winning. It's about playing the game."

Something in the man's warm, no-pressure invitation convinced Bob. He pulled out the chair and sat down.

"I'm Bob," he said, extending his hand.

"Walter," the man replied, his handshake firm despite his age, which Bob guessed to be mid-seventies, similar to him. "White or black?"

"Black," Bob decided. Let the more experienced player make the first move.

Walter nodded and rotated the board so the white pieces were on his side. His fingers, slightly gnarled with arthritis but steady, moved a pawn forward two spaces.

"So," Bob said as he considered his response, "do you come here often for chess?" He winced inwardly at how the question sounded like a pick-up line, but Walter just chuckled.

"Three days a week, weather permitting. Tuesday, Thursday, Saturday. Been doing it for about five years now, ever since I retired."

Bob moved his knight, the familiar shape comfortable between his fingers. "And how often do you find someone to play with? I mean, sitting here in a park waiting for an opponent seems a bit... optimistic."

Walter's eyes twinkled as his bishop slid diagonally across the board. "Every time."

"Every time? Really?"

"Never failed yet," Walter confirmed. "Sometimes, I wait an hour, sometimes, just minutes. But someone always comes along who either knows how to play or wants to learn."

Bob advanced a pawn, blocking Walter's bishop's path. "That's hard to believe."

"Cape May attracts all sorts. Tourists, locals, young, old." Walter moved another pawn, setting up a defensive position. "I've played against teenagers skipping school, college kids on break, business executives taking a mental health day, retirees like us. Even taught a few six-year-olds the basics."

Bob found himself relaxing into the rhythm of the game, memories of strategies and patterns resurfacing from some dusty corner of his mind.

"You're not as rusty as you claimed," Walter observed after Bob executed a clever move that put Walter's queen in jeopardy.

"Muscle memory, I guess," Bob replied, though he felt a small surge of pride. "My father was quite good. He used to say chess was life in miniature."

Walter nodded thoughtfully as he maneuvered his queen to safety. "Smart man, your father. The game teaches patience, foresight, consequences. Shows how a small move now can have big repercussions ten moves later."

They played in silence for a while, the only sounds being the gentle click of pieces against the board and the distant laughter of children playing. Bob found himself enjoying not just the game but the companionship too. There was something comfortable about sitting across from another man, focused on the shared challenge before them, no need for constant conversation.

"So, what brought you to Cape May?" Bob asked eventually.

"My wife and I had a summer home here for years. When I retired from teaching mathematics at Rutgers, we decided to make it our permanent residence." Walter's rook captured one of Bob's knights. "Jean still works part-time at the library. Says she's not ready to fully retire yet."

Bob nodded, impressed. "Good for her."

Walter smiled with evident pride. "She loves it here. Says the ocean air makes her feel alive. As for me, I needed something to get me out of the house, to connect with people while she's working. Chess seemed logical."

"And how do you handle playing with strangers?" Bob asked, moving his queen to a more aggressive position. "What if someone's a poor sport or tries to cheat?"

"You'd be surprised how rare that is," Walter replied. "Something about sitting face-to-face with another human being tends to bring out the best in people. We've forgotten that in this digital age—the power of looking someone in the eye."

Bob saw an opening and took it, capturing Walter's bishop. "Check."

Walter smiled and moved his king. "Good eye."

The game continued, becoming more complex as pieces were captured and the board opened up. Bob was fully engaged now, plotting several moves ahead, trying to anticipate Walter's strategy. He hadn't realized how much he'd missed this—the mental challenge, the quiet intensity of it.

"What about you?" Walter asked. "You and your wife live in Cape May year-round?"

"How'd you know I was married?"

Walter pointed at Bob's left hand. "Wedding ring. Well-worn."

Bob smiled. "Yes, we've always lived here in Cape May. Our daughters, Margaret and Liz, live here too. Margaret with her husband and our two granddaughters, and Liz with her husband and our two grandsons."

"Ah, family nearby. That's a blessing."

"It is," Bob agreed.

The game had reached a critical juncture. Bob had

Walter's king cornered, but Walter's queen and rook were threatening Bob's king as well. Bob studied the board, considering his options.

"So, what does your wife do while you're playing chess in the park?" Walter asked.

Bob moved his queen, committing to an aggressive approach. "Judy keeps plenty busy. She's always been good at finding interesting ways to spend her time."

Walter nodded appreciatively as he countered Bob's move. "Smart woman. The mind needs exercise just like the body. Check, by the way."

Bob frowned, seeing he'd overlooked a vulnerability. He moved his king to safety.

"The game itself keeps my mind sharp," Walter said.

Bob nodded then realized with a start that Walter had maneuvered him into a tight spot on the board.

Three more moves, and Walter declared, "Checkmate."

Bob studied the board, confirming Walter's victory, then extended his hand. "Well played."

"You gave me a run for my money," Walter said, shaking Bob's hand. "Especially for someone who hasn't played in years."

As they began resetting the pieces, Bob noticed a teenager hovering nearby, backpack slung over one shoulder, clearly interested in the game.

"Looking for a match?" Walter called to him.

The boy nodded, approaching shyly. "If you're not too busy."

"Perfect timing," Walter said. "Bob and I just finished."

Bob stood, offering his chair to the teen. "He's good," Bob warned with a smile. "Don't let his age fool you."

The boy grinned, sliding into the seat. "That's okay. I like a challenge."

Walter winked at Bob. "Tuesday, Thursday, Saturday. Early morning's usually best. Less competition for a seat."

"I'll be back," Bob promised, surprised to realize how much he was looking forward to it.

As he walked away, he glanced back to see Walter explaining something to the teenager, both of them leaning intently over the board. The scene warmed him somehow—the passing of knowledge, the connection across generations, the simple joy of a shared experience.

* * *

Judy pushed open the door to Seaside Haven, her third bookstore visit this week. The charming shop in Stone Harbor was about twenty minutes north of Cape May, but she'd heard good things and decided it was worth the drive. A small bell tinkled overhead, and she breathed in the comforting scent of books, coffee, and freshly baked pastries. This place was quickly becoming her favorite among the Jersey shore bookstores she'd been exploring.

"Good morning," the young woman behind the counter called out. "Let me know if you need any help finding something."

Judy smiled and nodded then began wandering through the shelves. She loved this part—the slow, meandering exploration, running her fingers along the spines, pulling out titles that caught her eye. The bookstore was arranged thoughtfully, with cozy reading nooks tucked into corners and small handwritten recommendation cards placed beneath select books.

She headed over to a corner of the store dedicated to reading accessories and gifts. Glass cases displayed artistic bookmarks with pressed flowers, sleek metal book lights that clipped onto pages, and scented candles with names like "Old Library" and "Rainy Day Reading." On nearby shelves, she found plush reading socks in autumn colors, delicate mushroom-shaped stickers, and notebooks decorated with painted succulents. She smiled, running her fingers over a particularly soft pair of burgundy socks. Maybe she'd treat herself on the way out.

After browsing the store some more, she finally came to the fiction section, where she found a historical novel set in Victorian-era Cape May that she'd been meaning to read. Moving on to the magazine rack, she selected three different publications—a travel magazine featuring coastal towns, a cooking magazine with fall recipes, and a gardening periodical with an article about preparing gardens for winter.

Arms full of reading material, Judy made her way to the café area. She ordered an Earl Grey tea and a cranberry-orange scone then found a plush armchair by the window that offered a view of the street.

"Perfect," she murmured to herself as she arranged her selections on the side table and settled in.

The scone was still warm, and she broke off a piece, savoring the sweet-tart flavor as she flipped through the travel magazine. Around her, Seaside Haven hummed with quiet activity—a college student typing furiously on a laptop, a young mother browsing picture books with a toddler in tow, the friendly barista creating elaborate latte art behind the counter.

Judy sipped her tea and watched people pass by the window, feeling a sense of contentment wash over her. There was something uniquely satisfying about carving out this time for herself, about the simple pleasure of good books, good food, and no particular agenda.

She picked up the cooking magazine next, lingering over recipes for pumpkin bread and apple cider donuts. She'd just turned to the historical novel when she sensed someone hovering nearby. Looking up, she saw a woman about her own age, silver-haired and stylishly dressed in linen pants and a light sweater, clutching a stack of magazines and a paperback.

"I'm sorry to bother you," the woman said, "but is anyone sitting here?" She gestured to the empty armchair adjacent to Judy's.

"Not at all. Please," Judy replied with a welcoming smile.

"Thank you. All the good spots fill up so quickly in here," the woman said, settling into the chair and arranging her reading materials on the table. "I'm Wendy, by the way. There's something comforting about being surrounded by books, isn't there?" Wendy gestured around the store. "Like being wrapped in a warm blanket of stories and ideas."

"I couldn't agree more," Judy replied. "I've become a bit of a bookstore addict lately. I've been exploring shops all over the Jersey shore whenever I get a chance."

"Oh? Which ones have you visited?" Wendy leaned forward, clearly interested.

"Well, there's Tidal Pages in Avalon—they have that wonderful mystery section. And Shoreline Books in Strathmere—smaller, but they serve the most delicious lavender shortbread with their tea. Then the Book Harbor in Cape May Point—they specialize in local history..."

They chatted easily, comparing notes on various bookstores they'd visited, both in Cape May and beyond. Judy learned that Wendy lived in Cape May as well and had been an English professor before retirement, specializing in nineteenth-century women's literature.

"I miss my students sometimes," Wendy admitted, "but I'm enjoying this chapter of life."

"I know what you mean," Judy replied. "Retirement has been wonderful."

They sipped their drinks in comfortable silence for a moment, each returning briefly to their reading. Judy found herself enjoying this unexpected companionship. Making new friends wasn't always easy, but there was something instantly familiar about Wendy, as if they'd known each other for years instead of minutes.

"Have you been to Maritime Pages over in Wildwood?" Wendy asked suddenly, looking up from her magazine. "I've heard they have an extraordinary collection of maritime literature."

Judy shook her head. "I haven't ventured over there yet. I'll add that to my growing list."

"We should go together," Wendy suggested, a spark of adventure in her eyes. "Maybe someday soon? I can drive, and we could make a day of it. Check out Maritime Pages and that little garden café that supposedly serves the best lemon pound cake on the Jersey shore."

Judy felt a flutter of excitement at the prospect. "I'd love that. It sounds like a wonderful adventure."

"Excellent," Wendy said, pulling a small notebook from her purse and jotting something down. "How's Saturday? We could leave around ten. Beat the lunch rush at the café."

They exchanged phone numbers and made tentative plans then returned to their reading, occasionally sharing an interesting passage or commenting on the comings and goings of other patrons. Judy was looking forward to Saturday with genuine anticipation. A new friend, a new bookstore, an adventure—small things, perhaps, but they made her feel vibrantly alive.

CHAPTER SIX

Margaret settled onto a bench at Lake Lily, placing her coffee, lunch, and the weathered shoebox beside her. The morning was crisp but pleasant, with golden sunlight filtering through the trees that surrounded the small lake. A few ducks glided across the water's surface, creating gentle ripples that caught the light. She'd been meaning to take time to properly explore the letters and diary she'd found, and this peaceful spot seemed perfect.

Dave was busy working at Pinetree Wildlife Refuge, and the girls were at school, while Margaret had just left the Seahorse Inn after checking in on things for the day—everything was running smoothly, per usual. Meanwhile, the beach house was coming along nicely—new plumbing, refinished floors in the living and dining room, and Dave had bought the supplies for the built-in bookshelves on either side of the fireplace and the mantel above it. But there was still so much to do, and they both needed occasional breaks from the constant work.

Margaret took a sip of her coffee then opened the shoebox and carefully untied the blue ribbon. She'd organized the letters by date during her lunch at Beach Plum Farm, which made it easier to follow William and Eleanor's story chronologically. She picked up where she'd left off, selecting a letter from winter 1953.

My dearest William,

As winter settles in, I find myself longing for summer and our cottage in Cape May. Teaching at the school just down the road from my parents' house has its advantages, but as you well know, it also means there's no escaping Mother's constant reminders of my "family obligations." The students are restless as the holidays approach, and I catch myself staring out the window during my planning periods, dreaming of salt air and the garden we'll plant come June.

Your letter about the bench you plan to build beneath the oak tree brought me such joy. I can already imagine sitting there in the evening, watching the fireflies emerge as darkness falls. How wonderful it will be to have those precious summer months in Cape May, where we can simply be ourselves without my mother appearing at my classroom door or your father summoning you to unexpected business meetings.

Mother cornered me after Sunday dinner yesterday. Her tone grows increasingly insistent that I give up my "foolish summer escapades," as she calls them, to focus entirely on family duties. Grandmother's health continues to decline, and my sister's children need looking after while she works at the family farm. Mother cannot understand why I insist on having "my own life" when family obligation should come first. I have not told her of our plans for the future. She would only redouble her efforts to keep me tethered here.

You mentioned your father's disapproval in your last letter. I worry about the strain it puts on you, defending our relationship to a man who measures worth only by family names and bank accounts. Sometimes I wonder if we will ever be free of their expectations—your family pulling you toward their vision of success, mine demanding my dutiful service.

Yet when I close my eyes and imagine us together again in Cape May, I know with certainty that we are making the right choice. Creating our own path, our own family, on our own terms.

The Christmas holiday approaches. Will you still be able to meet me at the cottage for those few precious days, or has your father scheduled more "important meetings" to keep you in Philadelphia? I pray the weather coop-

erates so we might have that time together before the long separation of winter stretches before us again.

Until then, I carry your heart with mine, Eleanor

Margaret felt a tightness in her chest as she refolded the letter. The challenges William and Eleanor faced were becoming clearer—family expectations pulling them in opposite directions from what they truly wanted. She selected another letter, this one from William to Eleanor, dated winter 1954.

My beloved Eleanor,

The holidays in Philadelphia have been particularly oppressive this year. Father's associates and their eligible daughters fill our home almost every evening for dinner parties I cannot escape. With each introduction, Father's intentions become increasingly transparent—to replace you in my heart with someone he deems more "suitable."

I find myself inventing excuses to retire early to my room, where I can at least imagine myself in Cape May, sitting beside you on the porch swing, listening to the distant sound of waves. Philadelphia has never felt less like home, nor our cottage more so.

I bring distressing news. Father has learned of my intention to relocate permanently to Cape May next summer. His reaction was precisely as we anticipated—first disbelief, then anger and finally a calculated attempt to change my mind. He has offered me a senior partnership in the firm, with a substantial increase in salary and responsibility. It is, in his words, "everything a young man of ambition could desire."

What he fails to understand, what he has always failed to understand, is that my ambitions lie elsewhere. I have no desire to spend my life among ledgers and contracts, attending endless dinners with people whose only measure of worth is financial success.

He spoke of you, Eleanor. Not kindly. He suggested that you have "turned my head" with romantic notions unsuited to a man of my position. When I defended you, he reminded me that your background is not what he had envisioned for his son's wife. As if your father's occupation could possibly diminish the brilliance of your mind, the generosity of your spirit, the depth of your character.

I left without resolving matters. For the first time in my life, I walked away from my father while he was still speaking. It felt both terrible and liberating.

I have been considering our options. Perhaps we should accelerate our plans. Why wait until spring? The cottage is ours. I have savings enough to sustain us while I establish a new career in Cape May. We need not live according to their timetables or expectations.

Write to me, my love. Tell me if I am being rash or if you, too, feel that the time has come to chart our own course, regardless of the storms that may follow.

Yours in heart and mind, William

Margaret lowered the letter, her coffee forgotten. The urgency in William's words, his determination to forge a path with Eleanor despite family opposition—it was so real, so immediate that it hardly seemed like decades had passed since he'd penned these words.

She glanced at her watch, realizing she'd been sitting there longer than she'd planned. But there was one more thing she wanted to examine before heading back—Eleanor's diary.

With careful fingers, she lifted the small leather-bound book from the bottom of the box. The pages were thin and delicate, yellowed with age. As Margaret began to read, she was drawn deeper into Eleanor's private thoughts.

Unlike the letters, which were carefully composed for William's eyes, Eleanor's diary entries were raw and unfiltered. They revealed the true extent of the pressure she faced from her family, particularly her mother, who saw Eleanor's summers in Cape May as a selfish indulgence when she should be helping with her ailing grandmother and her sister's children.

William's situation was equally fraught. His father, a prominent Philadelphia businessman, had specific expectations for his son that didn't include marrying a small-town schoolteacher or abandoning the family business to live in a beach cottage. The diary painted a picture of a young couple struggling against family obligations and social expectations, determined to forge their own path despite the obstacles.

But what really captured Margaret's attention was Eleanor's description of a treasure hunt William had created throughout Cape May. Apparently, he had hidden tokens of their relationship in various locations meaningful to them—a silver key beneath a specific boardwalk step, a porcelain bluebird buried in the garden, and even secret messages on cellar stones written in invisible ink that could only be revealed when held to a flame. There was also mentions of a jewelry box with a secret compartment and a map.

Margaret closed the diary, her mind racing. Could these things still be hidden in their beach house after all these decades?

She gathered the letters and diary then carefully returned them to the shoebox and secured the ribbon. This was no longer just a glimpse into a past romance—it was the beginning of a real mystery, one she could potentially solve.

* * *

"I'm looking forward to this musical tonight," Liz said as she and Margaret walked toward Tisha's, a few steps ahead of Dave and Greg.

"Me too. I've heard great reviews," Margaret replied. "And Tisha's was the perfect choice for dinner beforehand."

"Their seafood risotto is amazing," Liz said with a smile. "I might have to get that again."

Margaret nodded. "I've been thinking about it all day. Look, I think I see the others arriving."

They spotted Dave and Greg waiting near the entrance, Dave holding two bottles of wine they'd brought with them.

"There's the rest of our party," Dave said, nodding to the front door, where Sarah and Chris, Donna and Dale, and Nick and Lisa were walking in, chatting animatedly.

Tisha's was especially cozy tonight, with small tea lights flickering on each white-clothed table. The walls glowed warmly in the dim lighting, and the fragrant smell of garlic and herbs filled the air. The buzz of conversation created a pleasant backdrop to the intimate atmosphere of one of Cape May's most beloved restaurants.

"Your table is ready," the hostess said, gathering menus. "Follow me, please."

The five couples made their way through the restaurant to a large round table by the window. They settled in, exchanging greetings and compliments as they got comfortable.

"I brought a cabernet and a chardonnay," Dave said, placing the bottles on the table. "Anyone have a preference?"

"I'll start with the white," Donna said.

"Red for me," Sarah added.

A server brought over glasses and opened both bottles with practiced ease, then they passed the bottles around.

"The harvest salad is amazing," Lisa said, glancing at the menu. "Nick and I shared it last time we were here."

"And don't skip the arancini," Margaret added. "It's to die for."

After placing their orders, conversation flowed easily, punctuated by laughter and the occasional clink of glasses.

"So, what's new with everyone?" Liz asked then took a sip of her wine.

Sarah glanced around the table with a mysterious smile. "Well, I have news, but I've been sworn to secrecy until today."

All eyes turned to her expectantly.

"The Book Nook is hosting Blake Terry next week for the release of her new memoir."

"What?" Lisa's mouth dropped open. "Blake Terry? The Blake Terry? The Academy Award winner?"

"The very same," Sarah confirmed, unable to contain her excitement.

"How on earth did you manage that?" Dale asked, clearly impressed.

"Her publicist contacted me a month ago. Apparently, Blake has a soft spot for independent bookstores in small towns. They specifically requested Cape May for the East Coast leg of her tour."

"That's incredible," Donna said. "I loved her in that historical drama last year."

"When's the event?" Chris asked.

"This Monday evening," Sarah replied. "I just announced it publicly this morning, and we sold out all fifty seats within minutes."

"Only fifty seats?" Greg asked. "That seems like a small crowd for someone of that caliber."

Sarah sighed. "That's all the Book Nook can hold in our biggest room. I've had to turn down hundreds of requests already."

The server arrived with their appetizers—a harvest salad with roasted butternut squash, bleu cheese, and candied pecans; arancini served with marinara sauce; and a platter of fresh oysters. The conversation paused momentarily as they served themselves.

"This arancini is even better than I remembered," Dave said while dipping it in the marinara, then he took a bite.

Liz ate some of her salad then set down her fork. "Sarah, have you considered moving the event to a larger venue? What about the Cape May Movie Theater?"

Sarah's eyes widened. "I hadn't thought of that. But would they even consider hosting a book event?"

"It's worth asking," Margaret said.

"The theater can seat what? Three hundred people?" Dale asked.

"Just over three hundred in the main section, plus the balconies," Dave confirmed. "It would be perfect for an event like this."

Sarah bit her lip. "I don't know. The Book Nook is small, but it's intimate. And this would mean giving up my biggest event of the year."

"Not necessarily," Donna suggested. "Hold the talk and reading at the theater, then invite everyone to the Book Nook afterward for the signing and refreshments."

"That's brilliant," Lisa said, nodding enthusiastically. "You'd still get people in your store, but many more could attend the main event."

Their entrees arrived—seafood risotto for Margaret and Sarah, short rib Bolognese for Dave, sea scallops for Liz, and various other specialties for the rest of the table. The presentation was as impressive as the aromas that wafted up from the plates.

"Sarah, you should check with the theater manager after the show tonight," Greg said, cutting into his steak. "The worst they can say is no."

"I suppose it doesn't hurt to ask," Sarah agreed tentatively. "But what about ticket sales? The Book Nook event is already sold out."

"Refund those purchases and explain the change of venue," Dale suggested. "I bet most people would be thrilled about the switch."

"And charge a bit more for the theater seats," Liz added pragmatically. "The overhead will be higher."

Sarah took a sip of wine, considering. "I'll need to figure out logistics quickly if we're going to make this happen in less than a week."

"We'll help," Margaret assured her. "Between all of us, we can manage it."

By the time dessert arrived—a shared selection of crème brûlée, chocolate lava cake, and seasonal fruit with local honey—Sarah had warmed to the idea.

"I could host an after-party at the Book Nook," she mused.

"Nothing too fancy. Some wine, cheese, perhaps some hors d'oeuvres. Only those who purchase books would be invited."

"Perfect," Chris said. "You'd still have the intimate atmosphere for the serious fans."

Dave glanced at his watch. "We should probably head to the theater soon. Curtain's in thirty minutes."

They settled the bill, left a generous tip, and gathered their belongings. The night air was crisp as they stepped outside, the faint salt smell of the ocean mixing with the autumn scents of fallen leaves.

"Does everyone want to walk, or should we drive?" Dave asked, looking up at the clear night sky.

"Let's walk," Margaret suggested. "It's only a few blocks, and it's such a beautiful night."

The group strolled together down the street, couples walking hand in hand, their conversation drifting from Blake Terry's upcoming visit to speculation about the musical they were about to see.

As they approached the Cape May Movie Theater, its marquee illuminated the street with a warm golden glow. The historic building stood proudly on the corner, its facade restored to its original grandeur, with art deco flourishes and gleaming brass doors.

"I still can't believe how beautiful this place turned out," Dave said, admiring the theater as they approached.

"With your help," Margaret reminded him, squeezing his arm.

Inside, the lobby was even more impressive. They'd seen it already, of course, but it'd been a while since they'd been back. A crystal chandelier hung from the high ceiling, casting a gentle light over the marble floor. The walls were adorned with vintage movie posters in ornate gold frames, and the concession stand featured its original carved wooden counter, now polished to a high shine.

"Good evening, folks," the theater manager called out when he spotted them. "Dave, Margaret, great to see you!"

"James! Just the person we wanted to see," Dave replied. "Do you have a moment after the show? Sarah has a proposition for you."

"Intriguing," James said with a raised eyebrow. "I'll find you after the final curtain."

They made their way through the lobby to the main theater, where an usher checked their tickets and directed them to their seats. The interior was breathtaking—rows of plush red velvet seats faced a stage framed by thick crimson curtains with gold tassels. The ceiling was painted with a celestial mural, tiny lights embedded within to mimic stars, and ornate plasterwork adorned the walls and balconies.

"These are great seats," Greg whispered as they settled into the center section, about ten rows back from the stage.

The theater filled quickly, the excited murmur of the audience growing as showtime approached. At precisely eight o'clock, the house lights dimmed, and a hush fell over the crowd. The grand curtains parted slowly, revealing an elaborate set depicting a quaint New England town.

The musical was a revival of a classic Broadway show, with updated orchestrations that gave the familiar songs new life. The performers were outstanding, their voices filling the theater without the need for excessive amplification—a testament to the venue's superb acoustics.

During intermission, they gathered in the lobby for drinks.

"The lead actress is phenomenal," Donna said and sipped a glass of champagne. "Her voice gives me chills."

"The whole production is top-notch," Nick agreed. "I'm glad we made the effort to come out tonight."

"Much better than our usual Friday night of takeout and falling asleep on the couch," Lisa added with a laugh.

The second act was even more impressive than the first, building to an emotional finale that had several audience members dabbing at their eyes. When the final note faded, there was a moment of reverent silence before the theater erupted in applause. The cast took several bows as the audience rose to their feet for a standing ovation.

As the crowd began to disperse, James, the theater manager, approached their group.

"Enjoyed the show?" he asked.

"It was wonderful," Margaret replied. "The performers were incredible."

"Glad to hear it," James said then turned to Sarah. "Now, I understand you have something to discuss?"

Sarah explained the situation with Blake Terry and the limited capacity at the Book Nook.

"So you're wondering if we could host the event here instead?" James clarified.

"Yes, exactly," Sarah said. "It would be Monday evening. We'd need the stage set up for a reading and a Q and A session. I know this is very short notice and would totally understand if you can't do it."

James considered for a moment. "We don't have a show scheduled for that night, so the space is available. I've been wanting to branch out into more diverse programming anyway."

"That sounds promising," Sarah said cautiously.

"Let me make a call," James said, pulling out his phone. "I need to make sure I can get staff for that day."

He stepped away for a few minutes while the group waited anxiously.

"This could be huge for the Book Nook," Chris said to Sarah. "Even bigger than you originally planned."

James returned with a broad smile. "Everybody I called is free to work and excited to be a part of this huge event. I'd say this is a go."

Sarah's face lit up. "Really? That's amazing!"

"We'll need to work out the details—ticket prices, security, setup—but consider it booked. We'll have to move quickly with putting this together," James confirmed.

"I was thinking of hosting an after-party at the Book Nook," Sarah added. "For those who purchase the memoir. Would that work with the theater's policies?"

"Absolutely," James assured her. "We can even announce it during the event."

As they left the theater, stepping back into the cool night air, Sarah was practically vibrating with excitement.

"I can't believe this is happening," she said. "Blake Terry at the Cape May Movie Theater then an exclusive signing at the Book Nook. It's going to be the event of the year!"

"See what happens when we all get together for a night out?" Margaret teased. "Magic."

They walked back toward the restaurant where they'd parked their cars, the couples naturally falling into smaller conversations. The streetlights cast a warm glow on the brick sidewalks, and somewhere in the distance, they could hear the faint sound of the ocean.

"We should do this more often," Dave said, his arm around Margaret's shoulders.

"Absolutely," she agreed. "Though I doubt every date night will result in a celebrity book event."

"In Cape May? You never know," Dave replied with a smile. "That's the beauty of this place. You think it's just a quiet little town, then suddenly, you're helping restore a movie theater with a famous actress or hosting an Academy Award winner at the local bookshop."

Margaret laughed. "When you put it that way, it sounds absolutely ridiculous."

"Ridiculously perfect," Dave corrected, pulling her closer as they walked beneath the star-filled sky.

CHAPTER SEVEN

"I have an idea," Greg said as he sat across from Liz at their kitchen table, sipping his coffee. "Let's take a walk around town today. I want to get a feel for what's working for other businesses in Cape May."

Liz looked up from her sketch pad, where she'd been drawing out ideas for a china cabinet restoration. "Yeah? That actually sounds nice. I could use the fresh air, and I've been cooped up in the garage all week."

"Great. I'll pick you up around eleven?" Greg asked as he stood up to rinse his mug in the sink.

Liz laughed. "Pick me up? I'll be right here."

Greg smiled. "I mean I'll swing by after I finish up going over inventory at Heirloom. All the kitchen equipment, tables, chairs, et cetera. It'll be good to know when it's time to decide my new plan."

Liz nodded, understanding the weight of what Greg was going through. Heirloom had been his dream for years. "I'll be ready."

At eleven, Greg pulled up in front of their house and texted Liz he was outside. She appeared moments later wearing jeans and a light sweater, her hair pulled back in a loose ponytail.

"This feels silly," she said as she climbed into the passenger seat. "Like we're dating again."

"That's kind of the point," Greg replied with a grin. "I want today to feel fresh. New possibilities. A reset button."

As they drove toward town, Greg seemed more relaxed than Liz had seen him in months. The decision to close Heirloom, while painful, had lifted a visible weight from his shoulders.

"So, where to first?" Liz asked as they parked near the pedestrian mall.

"I thought we'd just wander. No agenda. Let's see what catches our eye."

They started at a small bakery tucked between a bookstore and a souvenir shop. The line was out the door, even though it was a Thursday in early fall.

"They only sell four things," Greg observed, examining the simple menu board. "Croissants, bagels, coffee, and freshly squeezed orange juice."

Liz watched as customers walked out clutching brown paper bags. "But they must do those four things really well."

"Exactly," Greg said, his eyes lighting up. "And look at their hours. Seven to two. That's it."

They continued down the street, stopping in a clothing boutique that specialized in coastal-inspired attire. The owner, a woman in her fifties, chatted with them about her business model.

"We're only open nine months a year," she explained. "We close January through March and travel. This year, we're going to Australia."

Greg nodded thoughtfully as they left. "Did you hear that? Nine months of work, three months of life."

They visited a coffee shop where local art hung on the walls with price tags, a hot dog stand that had been a Cape May institution for years, a plant store that doubled as a workshop space for gardening classes, a surf shop that rented equipment in the summer and sold custom boards year-round, and a jewelry store where the owner made pieces right in the shop window.

With each stop, Greg took mental notes, occasionally typing something into his phone. Liz found herself enjoying the adventure, seeing their familiar town through new eyes.

"What are you thinking so far?" she asked as they paused for lunch at a small sandwich shop.

Greg swallowed a bite of his turkey club. "I'm thinking that the most successful places here have three things in common. They're focused, they're authentic, and they know exactly what they're good at."

Liz nodded, considering his words. "And they all seem to have manageable hours."

By late afternoon, they had visited over a dozen businesses. As they headed back in the direction of Heirloom, Greg steered Liz toward Chocolate Days.

"One last stop. I want something sweet to end our field trip," he said.

Inside, Robby and June were arranging a new display case. When they spotted Greg and Liz, their faces lit up.

"Greg! You brought your better half this time," Robby said, coming around the counter to greet them.

"I've heard so much about your shop," Liz said, taking in the colorful displays of chocolates from around the world.

"Try this," June insisted, offering Liz a sample of dark chocolate with sea salt. "We just got it in from Ecuador."

As Liz savored the chocolate, Greg asked, "How do you two manage working together every day? As a couple, I mean?"

Robby and June exchanged glances.

"Oh, we have our moments," June admitted. "But honestly, it's the best decision we ever made."

"When we had the restaurant, we barely saw each other despite working in the same building," Robby explained. "I was in the kitchen. She was managing the front. We were like ships passing in the night."

"Now we actually work together," June added. "Side by side. And when we're done for the day, we're done. We close at five, and our evenings are our own."

Greg nodded, watching Liz as she browsed the chocolate displays. "And taking those long trips abroad? How do you manage that?"

"We plan for it," Robby said. "Save up, train a couple of part-timers to cover weekends, and for the rest, we just close. Customers understand. They wait for us to come back."

"That sounds amazing," Liz said, rejoining the conversation.

"Life's too short," June said, boxing up chocolates for them to take home. "This is on the house. Consider it inspiration."

After they left Chocolate Days, Greg suggested they walk over to Heirloom. The restaurant was closed for the day, but he unlocked the front door and led Liz inside. The familiar space felt different somehow, as if it already belonged to another life.

"Sit down," Greg said, pulling out a chair at one of the dining tables. "I want to talk to you about something."

Liz settled into the chair, watching as Greg took a deep breath.

"I have an idea for this place," he began. "A completely different vision from what Heirloom has been, but I think it could work. And I want you to be part of it."

"Me?" Liz asked, surprised. "What do you mean?"

Greg gestured around the restaurant. "What if we split this space in half? One side would be a showcase for your restored furniture. All those beautiful pieces you've been working on could be displayed here, for sale. You could add those ribbons and silk flowers you've been talking about, seasonal decor—whatever you want. The furniture would create these little vignettes throughout the space."

Liz looked around, suddenly seeing the potential. "And the other half?"

"A simple lunch spot. Nothing fancy. Sandwiches, salads, fresh juices, teas. Everything cold—no hot food and no dinner service. We'd close at four on weekdays, maybe seven on weekends. Limited menu, fewer employees, less stress."

Liz was quiet, taking it all in.

"I know you were hesitant about opening a store for your pieces," Greg continued. "But this way, you wouldn't have strangers coming to our home. It would give your work more exposure. People could still buy online, but they'd pick up here. And we'd be working together, side by side."

"Like Robby and June," Liz murmured.

"Exactly," Greg said, his excitement building. "We'd get home in time for dinner together. Eventually, with the right employees, we could even take weekends off. Maybe someday, long vacations like Robby and June do."

"And we wouldn't have to be there together all the time, right?" Liz asked, her practical side surfacing. "Some days, I could run the store while you take care of other things, and vice versa?"

Greg nodded enthusiastically. "Absolutely. We could set up a schedule where we overlap during busy hours but otherwise take turns. You could still have days to work in the garage on bigger restoration projects. I could have time to develop new menu items or handle the business side of things. It would give us both some independence while still working toward the same goal."

"I like that," Liz said. "It wouldn't feel like we're on top of each other all day, every day."

"Right. And when one of us needs a day off, the other could still keep things running. Much better work-life balance."

Liz stood up and walked around the space, visualizing it transformed. "It sounds wonderful, Greg. But the big question is: Would people come? Is there a need for this kind of business in Cape May?"

Greg joined her, taking her hands in his. "Honestly? We won't know unless we try. But think about what we saw today. Small, focused businesses, doing a few things really well. Owners who have time to live their lives. That's what I want for us."

Liz squeezed his hands. "It's a risk."

"So was opening Heirloom," Greg reminded her. "So was your quitting your job to restore furniture full-time."

Liz looked around the restaurant once more, imagining her refinished tables displayed with seasonal centerpieces, vintage hutches filled with treasures, and customers browsing while enjoying one of Greg's turkey sandwiches or fresh juices.

"What would we call it?" she asked, a smile spreading across her face.

Greg's eyes lit up. "I was thinking... Furnish and Feast."

"Furnish and Feast," Liz repeated, nodding slowly. "I like it. For the furniture, for the food, for us."

Greg pulled her close. "So are you in?"

Liz looked up at him, seeing the spark that had been missing for too long. "I'm in. Let's restore this place—and ourselves—together."

* * *

Days had passed since Nick submitted his offer on the bay house, and the waiting was slowly driving him insane. Every time his phone buzzed, he lunged for it, heart racing, only to be disappointed by spam emails or his mother asking if he'd seen her reading glasses. The Realtor had warned him it might take some time—the owner was out of state, dealing with a family emergency—but that didn't make the waiting any easier.

"You're going to wear a hole in my carpet," Lisa said, watching as Nick paced back and forth across her living room.

He stopped mid-stride, running a hand through his hair. "Sorry. I just can't stop thinking about it."

"I know," Lisa said, closing her laptop. She'd been trying to get some work done, but Nick's nervous energy was contagious. "You've checked your email twelve times in the last hour. I've been counting."

Nick dropped onto the couch beside her with a groan. "I put in a fair offer. Maybe even a little over what the place is worth, considering the work it needs. But what if someone else came in higher? What if there's a bidding war and I can't compete?"

"You don't know that," Lisa reminded him. "And worrying about it won't change anything."

Nick checked his phone again. Nothing.

"You know what?" Lisa said suddenly, standing up. "Let's go see it again."

Nick looked up, confused. "We can't. The lockbox code was only good for that one visit."

"I'm not saying we go inside. Just drive by. Maybe walk on the beach. It might help you remember why you want it so badly—or realize it's not worth all this stress."

Nick considered this for a moment then nodded. "Yeah, okay. Let's go."

He grabbed his keys from the coffee table, remembering the chaos he'd left behind at his own house. Since his parents had moved in with him, unable to afford their own place, they'd managed to fill every available space with their belongings. The third bedroom had become a storage unit for his mother's craft supplies, the shed where he used to find peace was now packed with his father's fishing gear, and he couldn't even make breakfast without navigating around his mother's extensive collection of decorative plates and magazines. With nowhere else for them to go, he'd made the difficult decision to let them stay in his house while he found a new place for himself. The cottage by the bay wasn't just a house—it was an escape, a chance to reclaim his space and his sanity without uprooting his parents.

* * *

The sun was just beginning to set as Nick's car bumped down the sandy lane toward the bay. The trees cast long shadows across the path, and the air was cooler here, carrying the tang of salt and the earthy scent of the marsh.

"It's even more beautiful at this time of day," Lisa remarked as the cottage came into view, its weathered shingles glowing gold in the slanting light.

Nick parked at the end of the lane, being careful not to block the driveway. The house was dark, the windows reflecting the sunset like burnished copper. Without the Realtor or the excitement of a first viewing, there was something almost magical about seeing the place now, quiet and still against the backdrop of the bay.

"Come on," Lisa said, hopping out of the car. "Let's check out your future beach."

They followed a narrow path that skirted the property line, making their way down to the shore. The tide was coming in, waves lapping gently at the sand. They found a large piece of driftwood bleached white by sun and salt and settled onto it side by side.

Nick took a deep breath, feeling some of the tension leave his shoulders. "This is exactly what I needed."

"I figured," Lisa said, bumping her shoulder against his. "Sometimes you need to reconnect with why you want something, not just obsess over whether you'll get it."

They sat in comfortable silence as the last sliver of sun disappeared below the horizon. The sky darkened, first to deep blue then to black, and stars began to appear—first just a few then dozens then hundreds, until the sky was a vast canvas of twinkling lights.

"Wow," Nick breathed, tilting his head back. "You don't see stars like this in town."

"No light pollution out here," Lisa agreed, following his gaze upward. "That's the Milky Way right there." She pointed to a misty band stretching across the sky.

In the distance, they could hear the occasional calls of shorebirds—the plaintive whistles of black-bellied plovers, the distinctive peeps of semipalmated sandpipers, and the harsh cries of a few lingering oystercatchers. The sounds blended with the rhythmic susurrus of waves on sand, creating a natural symphony that made Nick's heart ache with longing.

"If I get this place," he said softly, "I'm going to spend every night out here, just listening."

"Until winter," Lisa pointed out with a laugh. "Then you'll be inside by that fireplace."

"With a cup of something strong and hot," Nick agreed, smiling. "And maybe someone to share it with." He glanced at her then quickly looked away.

A sudden movement near their feet caught Lisa's attention. "Look!" she whispered, pointing at a small, pale shape scuttling across the sand.

A ghost crab, almost translucent in the moonlight, was making its way across the beach. It paused when Lisa pointed, seeming to consider them with its stalked eyes, then darted sideways and disappeared into a small burrow in the sand.

"They're everywhere once it gets dark," Nick said. "My dad used to take me ghost crab hunting when I was a kid. Not to hurt them—just to catch and release with flashlights."

"That sounds like fun," Lisa said. "Though I bet they're pretty quick."

"Lightning fast," Nick confirmed. "My success rate was about one in twenty. But the chase was the fun part."

The sound of voices drifted toward them from farther

down the beach. In the moonlight, they could make out two figures walking along the water's edge—a couple holding hands, bundled up in hoodies despite the mild evening. The pair nodded as they passed, their faces shadowed under their hoods, but their body language spoke of intimacy and contentment.

Nick watched them go, feeling a pang of something he couldn't quite identify. Envy? Longing? Hope?

"That could be you," Lisa said, seemingly reading his thoughts. "Morning walks before work, evening strolls after dinner."

"Yeah or even us," Nick agreed, his eyes still on the retreating couple. "That's what I want. Not just the house but the life it represents. Something peaceful. Something real."

Lisa felt something warm bloom in her chest, spreading outward until her fingertips tingled. She looked down at the sand, hoping the darkness hid the flush she could feel rising to her cheeks. When she finally spoke, her voice was soft. "It sounds perfect."

A cool breeze came off the water, making Lisa shiver slightly. Without thinking, Nick put his arm around her shoulders. She stiffened for just a moment then relaxed, leaning into him.

"I'm worried my offer won't be enough," he confessed, voicing the fear that had been gnawing at him. "This place is special. Other people must see that too."

"Your offer was fair," Lisa reminded him. "And sometimes it's not just about the highest bid. The owner might like the idea of selling to someone who'll really appreciate the place."

"And if I do get it, there's the mortgage to worry about. I'd be stretching myself pretty thin financially."

Lisa turned to look at him, her expression serious in the dim light. "Are you having second thoughts?"

"No," Nick said firmly. "No, I want this. I just need to figure out how to make it work." He gazed out at the bay, the surface rippling with moonlight. "I'd need to expand the oyster business. Find more restaurants, more clients. Maybe even pick up some shifts at Joe's Oyster Bar again."

"If anyone can make it work, it's you," Lisa said. "I've seen how you've built the farm up from nothing. You're resourceful."

Nick smiled, grateful for her confidence. "Joe's been asking me to come back anyway. Cover a few weekend shifts. Said his new guy can't tell a martini from a margarita. It wouldn't be a terrible thing, picking up some extra cash. Might even be fun."

"Plus, you'd get to keep your ear to the ground. Network with potential clients," Lisa added. "Chefs and restaurant owners are always at that bar."

"True." Nick nodded, feeling a plan begin to form. "I could bring samples. Use the opportunity to promote the farm."

The breeze picked up again, carrying with it the distant sound of a boat horn. Nick checked his watch, surprised to see how late it had gotten. "We should probably head back," he said reluctantly.

Neither of them moved immediately. The peace of the moment—the stars, the rhythmic sound of waves, the solid warmth of each other's presence was too precious to break.

"If I get this place," Nick said finally, "I'm going to build a firepit right here. Nothing fancy, just a circle of stones. Somewhere to sit on nights like this."

"With a cup of something strong and hot?" Lisa echoed his earlier words.

"With you by my side," he completed the thought, his voice soft.

This time, when their eyes met, neither looked away. In the moonlight, Lisa's face was half in shadow, but Nick could see the curve of her smile, the question in her eyes. Something shifted between them, a decision made in silence. Nick leaned in slowly for a kiss.

They walked back to the car in silence, each lost in their own thoughts. As they reached the top of the path, Nick turned for one last look at the cottage, its silhouette dark against the star-filled sky.

"It'll be yours," Lisa said confidently, following his gaze. "I can feel it."

Nick wanted to believe her. As he started the car and they began the drive back to town, he found himself planning as if it were already a done deal—where he'd put his surfboards, which wall would be best for a bookshelf, what color he'd paint the kitchen. If he focused on those details, he could almost ignore the knot of anxiety in his stomach and the persistent fear that this dream, like others, might slip through his fingers.

CHAPTER EIGHT

Donna arrived at the Cape May Point beach cleanup an hour earlier than the scheduled meeting time. She'd dressed in layers—a light long-sleeve shirt beneath her Save Cape May Beaches T-shirt, which Ella had distributed to the core volunteers after their discovery of the tire dump.

In a remarkably short time, they had managed to mobilize what Donna now surveyed with a mixture of pride and amazement: the parking lot was already half full, volunteers milling about with coffee cups in hand, organizing equipment, checking clipboards, and greeting one another with the easy familiarity of people united by purpose.

"There she is!" Ella called out, jogging over. Her clipboard had multiplied into three, and she had a walkie-talkie clipped to her belt. Dark circles underlined her eyes, but her smile was as energetic as ever. "Can you believe this turnout? And it's not even nine yet!"

Donna laughed, scanning the crowd. "Honestly? No. I thought maybe we'd get fifty people if we were lucky."

"Last count was at one twenty, with more confirming by the hour. We might hit two hundred by midmorning." Ella handed Donna a walkie-talkie matching her own. "You're team leader for the south quadrant. Jerry's got north, I've got central, and Faye's handling the staging area for the removed tires."

"Team leader? Ella, I've been to exactly one beach cleanup."

"And you were part of the group that discovered the environmental disaster, then you personally called half the business owners in Cape May." Ella's tone brooked no argument. "Besides, you know how to organize people from your years running the funnel cake shop."

Before Donna could protest further, a familiar voice called from behind.

"I still can't believe Colin is actually working out," Dale said, approaching with two travel mugs. He handed one to Donna, the warm ceramic welcome against her chilled fingers.

"I've finally got a manager, and he's handling it all like a pro. I think I can actually do other things while he's overseeing the restaurant," he continued, looking around at the activity with something between bewilderment and admiration. "When you said, 'big cleanup,' I pictured, you know, maybe thirty people with garbage bags. This looks like a military operation."

"Just wait until you see the tires," Donna replied. "How many layers did you wear? It gets hot out there once we start working."

Dale patted his jacket. "I came prepared. Don't worry. Where do you want me?"

"South quadrant," she decided. "With me. I'm apparently a team leader now."

At exactly nine o'clock, Ella climbed onto the back of a pickup truck belonging to the public works department and called for attention. The crowd, which had indeed grown to nearly one hundred fifty people, quieted remarkably fast.

"First, thank you all for coming on such short notice," she began. "What we discovered during our last cleanup is unprecedented in Cape May's history. For those who haven't seen it yet, we're dealing with hundreds of tires illegally dumped in our protected dunes over what appears to be several years."

Murmurs rippled through the crowd. Donna noticed many faces she recognized—not just the usual environmental volunteers but business owners from the boardwalk, servers from local restaurants, families who frequented her Wildwood funnel cake stand, even Principal Mercer from the high school, accompanied by what looked like half the environmental club.

"Originally, the city planned to bring in heavy machinery," Ella continued, "but after consulting with dune preservation experts, we've determined that would cause more harm than good. The weight of the equipment could further compact the tires into the sand and damage the dune structure that protects our community from storms."

She gestured toward the beach. "Instead, we're going old school. Human chains. We'll extract the tires manually and pass them from person to person to the collection point, where they'll be loaded into proper disposal trucks. It's more labor-intensive, but it protects the dunes."

Ella divided the crowd into teams, explaining the quadrant system and introducing the team leaders. She then gave a final reminder to everyone about the importance of today's work.

"One more thing before we start. This isn't just about cleaning up someone else's mess. This is about reclaiming our beach, our dunes, our community. Today, we're sending a message: Cape May takes care of its own."

A spontaneous cheer went up, and Donna felt an unexpected lump in her throat.

As the teams dispersed to their assigned areas, Donna led her group of about forty volunteers toward the southern end of the tire dump. The dunes rose before them, sea grass swaying in the ocean breeze. From a distance, the tires were barely visible—black crescents emerging from the sand like strange industrial mushrooms.

"I'm going to need a line of people from the dune edge to

the collection point," Donna instructed, falling more easily into the leadership role than she'd expected. "We'll rotate positions every thirty minutes so no one gets too tired in any one spot. The people actually digging out the tires have the hardest job, so we'll rotate those positions most frequently."

Dale, standing beside her, added, "And everyone needs to stay hydrated. There are water stations set up, but don't wait until you're thirsty. Drink regularly."

Donna smiled at him gratefully.

The work began slowly as they established their rhythm. The first tire took nearly fifteen minutes to extract as it had been buried deep, with only its edge visible. But as the team refined their technique, the pace quickened. Volunteers with shovels carefully dug around each tire, mindful of the delicate dune structure. Others gently worked the rubber free, sometimes having to cut away plant roots that had grown through the tires over the years. Once freed, the tires moved along the human chain, hand to hand, all the way to the collection point, where Faye's team stacked them for loading.

"Some of these have been here for years," one of the high school students remarked, pointing at a tire he'd just helped extract. The rubber was degraded, crumbling in places. "Look how it's breaking down."

"That's the real problem," Jerry explained, having wandered over from his northern quadrant to check on their progress. "As tires decompose, they release all sorts of chemicals into the environment. Some of them are known carcinogens."

"Who would do this?" another volunteer asked, passing a particularly large truck tire down the line. "It's just so... deliberate."

Donna had wondered the same thing since their discovery. This wasn't casual littering or even a one-time dumping. This represented years of systematic environmental abuse.

"The police and environmental protection agencies are

investigating," she answered. "Based on the types of tires, they think it might be connected to a commercial tire shop or auto repair business."

By midday, the sun beat down mercilessly, and sweat streaked the volunteers' faces. As predicted, the temperature had climbed, and most people had shed their outer layers. The human chains continued their steady work, though the pace had slowed somewhat with fatigue.

Then like a mirage in the desert, a row of brightly colored trucks appeared in the parking lot.

"Is that... Mario's Tacos?" Dale squinted toward the vehicles. "And Smokey's Barbecue? And the French Connection crepes?"

"Looks like our reinforcements have arrived." Donna grinned. She'd called in more than a few favors to arrange this.

Mario's Tacos was a popular food truck that normally did a brisk business at the farmers' market and local events. Smokey's BBQ was a favorite at summer festivals with their pulled pork sandwiches and smoked ribs, while the French Connection offered sweet and savory crepes that usually had long lines at the boardwalk. Today, however, they had all come to feed the volunteers, adding to the community support that was already evident from the coolers of drinks from the Corner Grocery, portable wash stations from the hardware store, and the port-o-potties provided by Chambers Construction Company that had been set up since early morning. Large canopy tents had also been donated and erected throughout the area, providing much-needed shade for the volunteers taking breaks from the increasingly hot sun.

"Break time!" Ella's voice crackled over the walkie-talkies. "One hour lunch break, everyone. Food and drinks in the main parking area."

The volunteers didn't need to be told twice. They made their way back from the dunes, faces flushed with exertion but spirits high. Donna noticed how people who had arrived as strangers now chatted easily, united by their shared labor.

"You arranged all this?" Dale asked as they approached the food trucks, where lines had formed but were moving steadily. Mario himself was efficiently assembling tacos with his two sons working the assembly line, while the smoky aroma from Smokey's BBQ filled the air, and the sweet smell of crepe batter cooking wafted from the French Connection's window.

"Just made a few calls," Donna said. "Once people heard what we were doing, everyone wanted to help. Mario and the others left their regular spots to be here. They all said it was the least they could do."

Dale looked at her with an expression she couldn't quite define—something between pride and revelation. "You know, I've never seen this side of the community. I know the restaurant customers, sure, but this..."

"I know what you mean." Donna nodded, accepting a plate of tacos with a grateful smile at Mario. "It feels different. Like we're part of something bigger than just our business."

They found a patch of grass under one of the large shade tents to sit on while they ate. Dale had opted for Smokey's pulled pork sandwich, while Donna balanced both a taco plate and a dessert crepe for later. The lines for food had been long, but all three trucks worked efficiently, and the wait gave volunteers a chance to rest their tired muscles in the welcome shade. From this vantage point, they could see the full scope of the operation: three human chains extending from different sections of the dunes to the collection area, where a growing mountain of tires awaited transport. A city dump truck had arrived and was being carefully loaded.

"We've pulled out over two hundred tires already," Jerry reported, dropping down beside them with his own plate. "At this rate, we might actually clear all of them today. Having so many volunteers makes a huge difference."

"I can't believe how many people showed up," Donna

replied, surveying the scene. "I was worried we'd need multiple cleanup days."

After lunch, the work resumed with renewed energy. The afternoon brought its own challenges as the easily visible tires had already been removed, leaving only those more deeply embedded. The human chains had to extend farther into the dune area, with careful steps placed only where environmental experts directed to minimize impact on the protected ecosystem.

Donna found herself working alongside a retired couple she recognized as regular customers at the boardwalk.

"We've been coming to this beach for forty years," the woman, Martha, told her as they wrestled an especially stubborn tire from the sand. "Got engaged right over there by the lighthouse. Brought our kids here every summer. Now our grandchildren too."

Her husband, Ron, nodded. "Never thought I'd be spending my retirement digging tires out of the sand, but here we are." Despite his words, his tone held no complaint—only determination.

By four o'clock, exhaustion had set in. Muscles ached, hands were blistered despite gloves, and even the most enthusiastic volunteers were flagging. Yet no one left. They had established a rhythm now—dig, extract, pass, stack—that continued with dogged persistence.

Ella's voice came over the walkie-talkie again. "The trucks are full. They're making a dump run and will be back in an hour. Let's push for another thirty minutes then call it a day."

Donna relayed the message to her team, who responded with tired but determined nods. She'd rotated through all the positions throughout the day and now found herself at the extraction point, working directly with the tires. Dale was two people down the line, his usually immaculate appearance transformed by a day of manual labor—hair tousled, face sun-reddened, clothes smeared with sand and the black residue that came off the degrading rubber.

"You know," he called to her as they worked on freeing an unyielding tire, "we should do something at the restaurant. A fundraiser maybe, for the ongoing cleanup efforts."

"That's a great idea," Donna agreed, surprised and pleased by his initiative. "Maybe a special menu item where proceeds go to the environmental commission?"

"I was thinking bigger." Dale grunted as they finally freed the tire. "A full event. Get other restaurants involved. Maybe set up your funnel cake stand. Make it a community thing."

Donna paused, hands still buried in the sand, and looked at her husband with a mix of surprise and delight. "I'd like that," she said simply, handing him the tire.

At five-thirty, Ella called an official end to the day's work. The volunteers gathered once more in the parking lot, tired but visibly proud. The collection area now held over six hundred extracted tires—the entire dump had been cleared.

"We did it!" Ella told the crowd, her voice hoarse but triumphant. "Thanks to your incredible effort, we've removed every single tire from the dunes today. The environmental commission didn't think it was possible to complete this in one session, but you proved them wrong."

The announcement was met with tired cheers. Donna looked around at the volunteers—neighbors, customers, and even a few former strangers who'd simply seen the call for help on social media—and felt a swell of emotion that caught her by surprise. They had accomplished in a single day what everyone thought would take several weekends.

"The city has already approved a restoration project," Ella continued. "Next month, we'll be replanting native dune grass and installing educational signage about the importance of these coastal ecosystems. I hope to see many of you there as well. Same time next month for the replanting?"

The chorus of affirmative responses was immediate and enthusiastic.

As the crowd began to disperse, Donna and Dale lingered for a few minutes, looking back at the dunes they'd worked so hard to save.

"You done good, Donna," Dale said quietly, the simple phrase carrying more weight than a flowery speech.

"We all did," she replied, leaning slightly against his shoulder, muscles aching in a way that felt earned... important.

The beach spread before them, bathed in late-afternoon light. Beyond the cordoned-off dune area, a few late-season tourists strolled along the water's edge, unaware of the day's massive effort. Soon, Donna thought, there would be no evidence of the tires at all—just healthy dunes protecting the shore, as nature intended.

She thought about her work, the business that had defined her over the past few years. It was still there, still important. But somehow, it no longer seemed like the only thing that mattered. There was room in her life for something more, something that connected her to this place and these people in a different way.

"You know," Dale said, interrupting her thoughts, "I don't think I've ever really looked at Cape May like this before. As something we need to protect, not just enjoy."

Donna nodded, understanding exactly what he meant.

"Same time next month?" she asked, echoing Ella's question.

Dale grinned, the expression transforming his tired face. "Wouldn't miss it."

As they walked back to their car, tired but satisfied, Donna felt something while searching through her belt bag. She reached in and pulled out the dried seahorse she'd found during that first cleanup. She'd completely forgotten she'd tucked it away.

"What's that?" Dale asked, peering at the tiny object in her palm.

"A seahorse I found on the first cleanup," she explained, studying its perfectly preserved form. "I meant to take it home that day, but then we discovered the tires, and everything else happened so fast."

She turned it gently in her fingers, admiring its fragile beauty.

Cape May was like that, too, she realized. Delicate in its natural beauty, vulnerable to human carelessness, yet surprisingly resilient when its community came together in its defense.

And so, perhaps, was she.

CHAPTER NINE

Judy checked her watch as she waited outside her house, a small woven tote bag slung over her shoulder. Right on time, a sleek blue sedan pulled into the driveway. Wendy waved from behind the wheel.

"Ready for our bookstore adventure?" Wendy called as Judy approached the car.

"More than ready," Judy replied, sliding into the passenger seat. The interior of Wendy's car was immaculate, with a faint scent of lavender hanging in the air. "I've been looking forward to this all week."

"Me too," Wendy said, backing out of the driveway. "I'm excited to visit Maritime Pages and then relax in their garden café."

As they drove north along the coast, conversation flowed easily between them, as if they'd known each other for years instead of just days. They shared stories about their lives before Cape May, their favorite books, and places they'd traveled.

The drive to Wildwood went smoothly, the scenery shifting gradually from Cape May's Victorian charm to Wildwood's more vibrant, colorful atmosphere. Wendy navigated the streets with confidence, turning down a quieter side road lined with small shops.

"There it is," she said, pointing ahead to a weathered blue building with white trim. A hand-painted sign swung gently in the breeze: Maritime Pages, with a small anchor decorating the *M*.

They found parking easily on the street and made their way toward the bookstore. Even from outside, Maritime Pages exuded character. The large front windows displayed an artful arrangement of books, nautical instruments, and model ships. Wind chimes made from sea glass tinkled softly above the entrance.

"Oh, look at this," Judy said, pausing at the doorway. Several colorful ceramic bowls sat on the ground beside the entrance, each filled with fresh water. Nearby, a wicker basket overflowed with tennis balls, and a small chalkboard sign read "For our four-legged friends. Help yourself! "

"Dog friendly," Wendy noted with approval. "I should have brought Marigold."

"You have a dog?" Judy asked, surprised they hadn't discussed this during their previous conversation.

"A golden retriever. She's getting on in years but still loves a good adventure," Wendy replied. "What about you? Do you have pets?"

"I have Hugo, a rather opinionated mutt," Judy said with a smile. "And Bruce, my orange cat who thinks he's in charge of the household. Hugo loves stores that offer treats, though Bruce prefers to stay home and nap in sunny spots."

"Next time, we should bring the dogs," Wendy suggested warmly. "I'd love to meet Hugo."

They pushed open the door and stepped inside. Maritime Pages was larger than it appeared from outside, with bookshelves stretching from floor to ceiling and narrow pathways winding between them. The space smelled of old paper, coffee, and something faintly salty—perhaps a sea-scented candle burning somewhere in the depths of the store.

"Welcome to Maritime Pages," called a cheerful voice. A woman with curly red hair and glasses perched on top of her head emerged from behind a counter. "I'm Amber. First time visiting us?"

"Yes," Judy replied. "We've heard wonderful things about your store."

"Well, feel free to explore. We specialize in maritime literature, of course, but we've got a bit of everything. The café is through the back door and into the garden. And if you have any questions, just holler."

"Thank you," Wendy said. "We'll definitely check out the garden café."

They began their exploration, meandering through the shelves with the unhurried pleasure of true book lovers. The maritime section was indeed impressive—everything from practical sailing manuals to fictional sea adventures, historical accounts of famous shipwrecks to coffee table books featuring underwater photography.

"Look at this," Judy said, pulling out a beautiful illustrated edition of *Moby Dick* with hand-drawn maps and detailed sketches of whaling equipment. "The craftsmanship is remarkable."

Wendy was equally enchanted by a collection of lighthouse photography and a slim volume of poems inspired by the sea. They moved slowly through the store, occasionally reading passages aloud to each other, their shared delight in discovery strengthening their newfound friendship.

Besides books, Maritime Pages offered an eclectic selection of nautical items—compass paperweights, bookends shaped like ship wheels, reading lights designed to look like vintage lanterns, and handcrafted jewelry made from sea glass and silver. Judy found herself drawn to a bookmark featuring a hand-painted lighthouse that reminded her of the one at Cape

May Point. "A little souvenir," she said as she added it to her growing stack of books.

After nearly an hour of browsing, their arms laden with books and treasures, they made their way to the checkout counter. Judy purchased her lighthouse bookmark, a historical novel about shipwrecks along the Jersey coast, and a book of sea-inspired poetry. Wendy selected several nautical mysteries and a beautiful coffee table book featuring lighthouses of the Eastern Seaboard.

With their purchases securely bagged, they made their way toward the back of the store. A glass door opened onto a surprisingly spacious garden, where tables and chairs were scattered beneath the shade of large canvas umbrellas. Several people sat reading or chatting quietly, and two dogs—a chocolate lab and a small white terrier—played a gentle game of tug-of-war with a rope toy in a corner of the yard.

"This is perfect," Wendy said, spotting an empty table near a small burbling fountain. "Why don't you grab the table, and I'll order for us? What would you like?"

"I'll try their seasonal tea," Judy replied. "Something with autumn spices if they have it. And definitely a slice of that famous lemon pound cake. I've been looking forward to trying it since you mentioned it. For something savory, I'll have whatever you're having."

While Wendy headed to the small counter at the edge of the garden, Judy arranged their books on a rustic wooden table and settled into a comfortable chair. The garden was lovely—not overly manicured but thoughtfully designed with potted herbs, climbing roses, and strings of tiny lights that would surely create a magical atmosphere in the evening. She watched a monarch butterfly flutter from flower to flower and felt a sense of deep contentment wash over her.

Wendy returned a few minutes later, carefully balancing a tray loaded with teapots, cups, and several plates of food.

"A spiced apple cinnamon tea for you," she said, setting

Judy's teapot down. "It's their autumn special. I ordered us each a crab salad sandwich and, of course, slices of the lemon pound cake we've been hearing so much about. I also got us each a cup of their seafood chowder to start."

"This looks wonderful," Judy said, pouring her tea. The rich aroma of apples and warm spices rose with the steam, and she breathed it in appreciatively. "What a find this place is."

They ate slowly while glancing at their books, savoring both the food and the peaceful surroundings. The chowder was exceptional—creamy and rich with chunks of fresh fish and impeccably cooked potatoes. The sandwiches were equally delightful, with generous portions of fresh crab meat and crisp vegetables on sourdough bread. But it was the lemon pound cake that truly lived up to its reputation—moist and buttery with a delicate balance of sweetness and a citrusy tang, topped with a thin lemon glaze that crackled pleasantly between their teeth.

"Oh my," Judy said after her first bite of cake. "That might be the best pound cake I've ever tasted."

"Isn't it divine?" Wendy agreed, savoring her own piece.

"I think I've found a new favorite spot," Wendy said, leaning back in her chair. She had bought a nautical mystery about a detective solving crimes along the New Jersey coast and was already a few pages in. "I could stay here all day."

"Me too," Judy replied, looking up from her own book—a collection of sea-inspired poetry. "It makes me wish I'd brought Hugo. He would love this garden."

"We'll definitely bring the dogs next time," Wendy said. "Marigold would enjoy those tennis balls by the entrance."

They read in companionable silence for a while, occasionally sharing an interesting passage or commenting on the comings and goings of other patrons. A soft breeze rustled the pages of their books and carried the scent of roses from a nearby trellis.

As the afternoon stretched on, they reluctantly gathered

their purchases, thanked Amber for her hospitality, and made their way back to Wendy's car.

"Where should we go in a week or two?" Wendy asked as they drove back toward Cape May. "I heard there's a wonderful little place in Ocean City that specializes in thrillers. They also have a charming tea room with literary-themed desserts."

"That sounds fabulous," Judy replied, her mind already spinning with anticipation. She glanced at Wendy, feeling a wave of gratitude for this new friendship. "Thank you for today. It was exactly what I needed."

"Me too," Wendy said, her eyes crinkling with a smile. "I think we've found something special here—not just the bookstores, but this..." She gestured between them. "This friendship. I'm looking forward to many more adventures."

"Absolutely," Judy answered, already thinking about exploring more literary havens along the Jersey shore. At this stage of life, finding a kindred spirit was a rare and precious gift—one to be treasured like a first edition or a cup of tea on a rainy afternoon. "Many more adventures to come."

* * *

Bob arrived at Rotary Park earlier than he had for their previous game, hoping to get there before Walter. To his surprise, Walter was already seated at the chess table, pieces arranged perfectly, deep in thought as he studied the board.

Walter looked up, and his face broke into a wide smile when he spotted Bob approaching. "Good morning! I had a feeling you might return soon."

"Looks like I wasn't early enough," Bob said, taking the seat opposite Walter. "How long have you been here?"

"Oh, not long," Walter replied, though the half-empty thermos of coffee beside him suggested otherwise. "I enjoy the morning stillness. Gives me time to think."

As Bob settled in, he felt a quiet confidence. The hours spent watching instructional videos and playing against computer opponents since their last game had reawakened skills long dormant. He wasn't just relying on muscle memory anymore.

"I see you've set me up with white today," Bob noted, gesturing to the board.

Walter nodded. "Thought you might like to take the offensive this time."

"I've been practicing," Bob admitted.

Walter's eyes twinkled. "Online?"

Bob nodded. "There's an entire universe of chess content out there. I had no idea until I started looking."

"There certainly is. Though I still prefer the feel of real pieces and a real opponent across the table." Walter gestured to the board. "Your move."

Bob opened with the queen's pawn game, advancing his pawn to d4. Walter responded quickly, matching with his own pawn to d5. The game was on.

As they played, Bob was more conscious of his strategy, thinking several moves ahead instead of just reacting to Walter's plays. He'd deployed the opening he'd studied most carefully, establishing control of the center of the board while developing his bishops and knights methodically.

Walter raised an eyebrow after Bob's sixth move brought his knight to a threatening position. "Someone's been doing their homework," he commented.

"Just refreshing my memory," Bob replied modestly, though he felt a flush of pride.

They settled into the middle game, each man focused on the board. Bob found himself calculating possibilities with a clarity he hadn't felt in years. The mental exercise was exhilarating.

"How long have you been playing?" Bob asked during a brief pause while Walter considered his next move.

"Since I was eight," Walter replied, eyes still on the board. "My grandfather taught me. He was a postal worker who played chess by mail with opponents across the country. Sometimes, a single game would take months."

"Chess by mail? I can't imagine the patience required."

Walter smiled. "Different era. No internet, no instant gratification. You had to learn to wait, to live with uncertainty." He moved his bishop decisively. "What about you? When did you learn?"

"My father taught me when I was ten," Bob said, studying the new position on the board. "We played regularly until I left for college. After that, life got busy."

Walter nodded understandingly. "It happens. Family, career—priorities shift. But the game waits for us to return." He gestured toward the board. "And when we do come back, we find it's still there, unchanged yet always new."

As they talked and played, Bob noticed a few people pausing to watch. An older couple stopped on their morning walk, the woman whispering something to her husband as they observed. A young mother with a stroller lingered, absently rocking her sleeping baby while her eyes followed the movement of pieces. A teenage boy stood at a respectful distance, his hands shoved into his pockets, gaze fixed on the board.

Walter seemed to grow more methodical as spectators gathered, taking longer with each move, his brow furrowed in concentration. Bob recognized that he was facing a more determined opponent than in their first game.

"You're making me work today," Walter said after a particularly effective move by Bob.

"Just trying to keep up," Bob replied, though he knew he was doing more than keeping up—he was winning.

The small crowd had grown to about a dozen people, standing in a loose semicircle around the table. A man in his forties with a Red Sox cap leaned over to his companion.

"White's got the upper hand now," he whispered loudly enough for Bob to hear.

"You play?" Walter asked him, looking up briefly.

The man nodded. "Club player. Nothing special."

"Feel free to join us next time," Walter offered. "Saturday mornings are usually best."

Bob smiled at Walter's ever-present invitation. The man truly believed in the community of the game.

Walter made a bold move with his knight. It was clever—the kind of multifaceted attack Bob might have missed before his recent study. But now he saw not only the immediate threat but also the strategy behind it.

"Interesting choice," Bob murmured, studying the board carefully. He looked up to find Walter watching him, a hint of challenge in his eyes.

Someone in the crowd whispered, "Black's in trouble now," and another voice responded, "No, look at white's exposed flank."

Bob tuned them out, focusing on the position before him. After careful consideration, he made his move.

A murmur ran through the onlookers. Walter's eyebrows rose slightly, and he nodded in appreciation before returning his attention to the board.

"Either you've been playing in secret all these years, or you're a very quick study," Walter commented.

Bob smiled. "Let's just say I had a good reminder of how much I enjoy the game."

The game had reached its critical phase. Pieces had been exchanged, the board more open now, each move carrying greater consequences. Bob felt sweat beading on his forehead despite the cool air. His heart beat a little faster as he recognized the approaching endgame.

"Ever play in tournaments?" Walter asked, perhaps as a distraction technique.

"Never had the nerve," Bob admitted. "You?"

"A few local ones, years ago. Won some, lost more." Walter moved his rook, capturing one of Bob's pawns. "Check," he announced.

Bob moved his king to safety then immediately made his countermove. "Check," he responded.

Walter had no choice but to move his king, which left his queen vulnerable. When Bob captured it two moves later, a ripple of excitement passed through the audience.

"Well played," Walter said, studying the board with a rueful smile. His king was now in a precarious position, with few escape routes remaining.

Bob advanced methodically, careful not to let overconfidence lead to carelessness. Walter defended skillfully, making Bob work for every advantage. But the outcome was becoming inevitable.

"Checkmate in three," someone in the crowd said quietly.

Walter saw it too. He looked up at Bob with respect in his eyes. "I believe this is yours," he said, offering his hand.

Bob reached across and shook it firmly. "Thank you for the game."

A smattering of applause broke out from the onlookers. Bob felt a flush of embarrassment mixed with pleasure. He hadn't played for an audience in—well, ever, really. Chess had always been a private pursuit for him.

"That was quite a match," said an elderly man as the crowd began to disperse. "You two play like professionals."

"Hardly." Walter laughed. "But we enjoy the game."

As they reset the pieces, a young woman with a small boy of about seven approached the table. "My son was watching your game," she said. "He's been asking to learn chess. Would either of you be willing to teach him sometime?"

Walter looked at Bob, a question in his eyes.

"I think between the two of us, we could manage some lessons," Bob found himself saying. "Maybe Saturday mornings?"

Walter beamed. "Perfect. I'm here Tuesdays, Thursdays, and Saturdays anyway."

The woman thanked them profusely while her son gazed at the chess pieces with fascination. After they left, promising to return Saturday, Walter turned to Bob.

"Teaching's as rewarding as playing, in its own way," he said. "Especially with the young ones. Their minds are so open, so quick to grasp new concepts."

Bob nodded, remembering teaching his own daughters to play when they were small. Liz had taken to it immediately, while Margaret had preferred more active pursuits. "I haven't taught anyone in years, but I'm willing to try."

"That's all any of us can do," Walter said, placing the last piece in position. "Try our best with what we know." He looked up at Bob with a smile. "Same time next week for our rubber match?"

"I wouldn't miss it," Bob replied, realizing he meant it. This unexpected friendship, formed over a chess board in a park, had already become something he valued. It wasn't just about the game—though the intellectual challenge was certainly appealing—but about the connection as well, the shared experience across the board.

As Bob drove home, he found himself thinking about Walter's chess philosophy. It wasn't just about winning; it was about the joy of the game itself, too, about the human connection formed when two minds engaged in this ancient battle of strategy and foresight. And now it would also be about passing those lessons on to the next generation.

CHAPTER TEN

The crisp afternoon had brought a pleasant breeze through the upstairs windows of the beach house. Margaret stood in the closet of the smallest bedroom, paintbrush in hand, carefully applying a second coat of soft cream paint to the interior walls. The fresh paint smell mingled with the scent of the wood stain Dave was using downstairs on the built-in bookshelves and new mantel that now flanked the fireplace.

From the screened-in porch below, Margaret could hear Harper and Abby's voices—Harper reading aloud from her latest fantasy novel while Abby occasionally interjected with questions or comments. The girls had been surprisingly content to spend the afternoon lounging on the wicker furniture, alternating between their books and tablets while Margaret and Dave continued their renovation work.

"Mom, can we help with anything?" Harper called up.

Margaret leaned out of the closet. "I think we're okay for now. Focus on getting your school reading done. We'll have some tasks for you next time."

"Okay!" Harper replied, her voice already fading as she returned to her reading.

Margaret smiled to herself. After their time working on the

beach house without the girls, it felt right to have them here, making the space truly theirs. Though the house was still very much a work in progress, enough had been accomplished that the renovation was taking shape. The new plumbing worked flawlessly, the newly finished hardwood floors had a subtle sheen, and the kitchen cabinets had been transformed with sanding and a rich mahogany stain.

She turned back to her painting, focusing on the top corner of the closet. As she stretched to reach it, her foot pressed against a floorboard that gave way slightly with a distinctive creak. Margaret paused, looking down. She pressed her foot against the board again, feeling it shift.

Setting her paintbrush across the top of the paint can, she knelt down for a closer look. The board definitely seemed loose. She ran her fingers along its edge, feeling a slight gap where it met the adjacent board. Curious, she pressed her fingertips into the gap and gently pulled upward. The board rose with surprising ease.

"What have we here?" she murmured, peering into the narrow space under the floorboard.

There was something there—a box of some kind, pushed back toward the wall. Margaret lifted another adjacent board, which also came up without much resistance. With both boards removed, she could see a metal box about the size of a shoe box tucked into the space between the floor joists.

Margaret reached in, her heart quickening as her fingers closed around the cool metal. She carefully extracted the box, noting its weight and the thin layer of dust that covered its surface. It was an old metal recipe box, the kind people used before digital recipe collections and Pinterest boards. The lid was decorated with a faded painting of fruit and flowers.

Setting it on the closet floor beside her, Margaret hesitated, feeling a tremor of excitement. First the letters and diary and now this. The beach house seemed determined to reveal its secrets bit by bit, like a slowly moving treasure hunt across time.

She lifted the lid, and her breath caught. Inside, meticulously organized and separated by small cardboard dividers, was a collection of photographs—dozens of them, each one carefully labeled with dates and names in elegant handwriting that Margaret instantly recognized from the letters and diary.

"Oh my goodness," she whispered, lifting out the first photograph.

It was a black-and-white image of the beach house itself, dated June 1951. The caption, written in the same flowing script as Eleanor's diary, read "Our summer cottage, first day." The house looked much the same as it did now, though the trees surrounding it were smaller, and the garden was far more developed, with neat flower beds and trimmed shrubs.

Margaret extracted another photo. This one showed a young couple standing on the front porch, arms around each other, faces illuminated with joy. "William and Eleanor, Fourth of July celebration, 1952." William was tall and lean with dark hair swept back from his forehead, wearing light-colored trousers and a short-sleeved button-down shirt. Eleanor was tall with shoulder-length curled hair, wearing a full-skirted summer dress with a cardigan draped over her shoulders.

Margaret's fingers trembled slightly as she looked at their faces for the first time. After reading their words and feeling their emotions through the letters, seeing them in the flesh, even in a decades-old photograph, felt intensely personal, as if she were finally meeting dear friends she'd known only through correspondence.

She carefully sorted through more photos, finding images that chronicled their summers in Cape May. There were pictures of the garden in full bloom, with Eleanor kneeling beside rosebushes or William proudly displaying a newly planted tree. There were beach pictures—the two of them with friends, splashing in the waves, or lounging on blankets under striped umbrellas.

Then Margaret came across a stunning photo of the backyard. "Garden completion, August 1953" read the caption. The image showed the garden in its full glory—lush flower beds, a small vegetable patch, and there, beneath the oak tree, was the bench William had mentioned building in his letter. It was a simple wooden bench with curved armrests, positioned strategically to catch the dappled shade.

"The bench," Margaret whispered. "He really did build it."

She continued through the collection, finding a series of photos documenting dinner parties held in the house. One showed the dining room table set with fine china and candles, another captured William and Eleanor with four friends, glasses raised in a toast in the living room—the very same room where Dave was now working on the bookshelves and the mantel over the fireplace.

"William and Eleanor's first dinner party, July 1952" read one caption. The photo showed the couple standing in the kitchen, Eleanor in an apron, William holding a serving dish, both of them laughing, as if they'd just shared a private joke.

A particularly striking photo made Margaret pause. It showed William and Eleanor at what appeared to be a formal ball in Cape May. Eleanor wore a full-length gown with a fitted bodice and a full skirt, her hair styled in an elegant updo. William was handsome in a classic tuxedo, his hair slicked back. They were captured mid-dance, looking into each other's eyes with such palpable affection that Margaret felt like an intruder simply by viewing the image.

"Cape May Summer Ball, August 1954" read the caption.

There were more casual images too—William and Eleanor at what must have been a public pool, lounging on deck chairs, wearing the modest bathing suits of the 1950s and dark sunglasses. "Beach Club, July 1954," the back of the photo noted.

As Margaret continued through the collection, she noticed the photos becoming sparser as she reached 1955. And then she found one that made her heart skip a beat. It was a simple, intimate photograph of just their hands—Eleanor's slender fingers intertwined with William's larger ones. On Eleanor's ring finger was a diamond ring catching the light.

The caption read simply: "Our engagement, September 1955."

Margaret stared at the photo, a smile spreading across her face. They had gotten engaged. Despite the family pressures and obstacles they'd written about in their letters, William and Eleanor had committed to a future together.

But as she sifted through the remaining photos, Margaret realized there were no more after that date. The engagement photo was the last one in the collection. What had happened to them after their engagement? Had they married? Lived in the house year-round as they'd planned? Or had something prevented their happy ending?

"Margaret? You up there?" Dave's voice called from downstairs, breaking her reverie.

"Yes, in the closet!" she called back. "Dave, you need to come see what I've found!"

She heard his footsteps on the stairs then crossing the bedroom floor.

"What's going on?" he asked, appearing at the closet doorway. He had a smudge of wood stain on his forearm and another on his T-shirt.

"Look," Margaret said, gesturing to the open box and the loose floorboards. "I found these hidden under the floor."

Dave's eyes widened as he knelt beside her, careful not to knock over the paint can. "More treasures from William and Eleanor?"

Margaret nodded, selecting a few key photos to show him. "This is them. And this is the house back then. And look, here's the garden bench he mentioned building in that first letter I read."

Dave examined the photos with interest. "They look so happy. And young."

"They were," Margaret said, showing him more pictures of their dinner parties and outings. "It seems like they really loved this place. And look—they got engaged in September 1955."

She handed him the photo of their hands with the ring.

"That's wonderful," Dave said. "So they did end up together."

"Not sure," Margaret said, frowning slightly. "There aren't any photos after the engagement. Nothing about a wedding or their life afterward. It's like their story just... stops."

Dave handed the photos back to her. "Perhaps there's another box somewhere. Or maybe they moved away after getting married."

"Maybe," Margaret agreed, though she couldn't shake the feeling that there was more to the story. "I wish I knew what happened to them."

Dave stood and offered his hand to help her up. "The mystery continues. But hey, I came up to tell you I've finished staining the bookshelves and the new mantel. Want to come down and see?"

As Margaret carefully gathered the photos and returned them to the metal box, she replied, "Absolutely. Let me just put these somewhere safe until we can go through them properly."

She placed the box on the highest shelf in the closet, making a mental note to return to it later. The loose floorboards, she left as they were—a secret entrance to a hidden space that might contain more treasures.

As she followed Dave downstairs, Margaret couldn't stop thinking about William and Eleanor, now with faces to match the heartfelt words she'd read. Their love story had become even more real, more tangible, but the mystery of their fate lingered. What had happened after their engagement? Had they enjoyed a long, happy life together in this house, or had their story taken an unexpected turn?

* * *

The smell of grilling hamburgers and the sound of laughter filled the air as Margaret and Dave arrived at Donna and Dale's backyard with Harper and Abby in tow. The evening had turned cool, but Dale had set up two patio heaters around the deck, creating a comfortable bubble of warmth for their impromptu gathering. Strings of white lights zigzagged overhead, casting a soft glow on the friends who had already assembled.

"There they are!" Donna called, waving from beside the outdoor bar, where she was mixing a pitcher of something fruity. She wore jeans and a thick cream sweater, her hair pulled back into a casual ponytail. "We were starting to think you'd gotten lost in that renovation project of yours."

Margaret smiled as she set down the plate of brownies she'd brought. "Almost. We had the girls with us at the beach house today and lost track of time."

Harper and Abby quickly spotted the other kids inside and, after a quick greeting to Donna and Dale, headed into the house to join them.

Dave placed a six-pack of craft beer on the counter. "Sorry we're late. The staining and painting today took longer than expected."

Dale looked up from the grill, spatula in hand. "No worries. Burgers are just about ready." He gestured toward the gathering. "Everyone's here except Nick and Lisa, but they texted they're on their way."

Margaret scanned the yard. Greg and Liz stood near the firepit, deep in conversation with Chris. Sarah sat in an Adirondack chair, nursing what looked like a glass of wine, her expression pensive. Through the sliding glass door, Margaret could see the kids sprawled in the living room—Harper and Abby had immediately joined their cousins, Steven and Michael, along with Chris's son, Sam. They appeared to be engrossed in a movie, occasionally reaching for the bowl of popcorn on the coffee table.

"Here, take this," Donna said, handing Margaret a glass of sangria. "You look like you could use it after a day of painting."

"How did you know I was painting?" Margaret asked, accepting the drink gratefully.

Donna pointed at a small spot of cream-colored paint on Margaret's wrist that had somehow escaped her post-work shower. "Detective skills," she said with a wink.

As Margaret and Dave made their way around, greeting everyone, the sliding door opened, and Nick and Lisa hurried onto the deck, looking windblown but happy.

"Sorry we're late!" Lisa called out. "We got held up on a call with the Realtor."

"Perfect timing," Dale responded, lifting the first batch of burgers from the grill. "Food's ready."

They all gathered around the large outdoor table, passing dishes of potato salad, coleslaw, and corn on the cob. For a few minutes, conversation lulled as everyone filled their plates and settled in to eat.

"So," Donna said once everyone had taken their first few bites, "what's this big news you've been hinting at all day, Greg? You've been practically bursting since you got here."

All eyes turned to Greg and Liz, who exchanged glances before Greg cleared his throat.

"Well," he began, setting down his burger, "we're moving forward with our new venture."

"The one you've been brainstorming?" Chris asked between bites.

Liz nodded, excitement lighting up her face. "We've finalized the plans for transforming Heirloom. We're calling it Furnish and Feast."

"So it's official?" Margaret asked.

"Signed the paperwork yesterday," Greg confirmed. "A complete reimagining of the space. We're dividing it into two connected businesses—a showcase for Liz's furniture pieces on one side and a casual lunch spot on the other."

"What made you decide to take the plunge?" Dale asked.

Greg's eyes met Liz's briefly. "Life's too short to stay in a business that's draining us. The fine dining world was becoming more stress than joy."

"And now I'll have a real showroom for my furniture," Liz added. "A professional space where customers can see the pieces in room settings instead of just photos online. Plus, we'll be involved in the business together but on our own terms."

"The menu will be completely different," Greg continued. "No more dinner service. No more elaborate preparations. Simple lunches, quality ingredients, everything served cold so we can prepare ahead. We'll close by mid-afternoon most days."

"To Greg and Liz," Dale said, raising his beer bottle. "And to taking chances on dreams."

Everyone lifted their glasses in a toast, and the couple beamed.

"Speaking of taking chances," Nick said as the toast concluded, "I have some news too." He glanced at Lisa with a smile. "My offer on the bay house was accepted today."

Another round of cheers went up.

"The cottage by the bay?" Sarah asked, momentarily distracted from her thoughts about the Blake Terry event.

Nick nodded, clearly excited. "It needs work, but the location is perfect, and the views are incredible. I close in thirty days."

Lisa gave his arm a supportive squeeze, remembering how his face had lit up when they'd first walked the property together and he'd seen the view of the bay.

"Congratulations!" Margaret said. "Looks like Dave and I won't be the only ones knee-deep in renovation dust."

"If you need help with anything, just let me know," Dale offered. "I've got that tile saw you might need for the bathroom."

"Same. I'm a phone call away," Greg said with a smile.

Chris frowned and looked at the large walking boot on his foot. "Wish I could help. If you need someone to sit in the corner and tell jokes, I'm your guy," he said with a chuckle.

Everyone burst out laughing.

There was a momentary lull in the conversation, and Margaret noticed Sarah fidgeting with her napkin, her earlier pensive look returning. "Sarah, everything okay? You've been quiet tonight."

Sarah looked up, seeming almost startled to be addressed directly. "Oh, I'm fine. Just a complete bundle of nerves about tomorrow."

Chris reached over and squeezed her hand. "As you know, Sarah's preparing for Blake Terry's book event at the Cape May Movie Theater. She's been working on it nonstop."

Sarah nodded. "I just can't believe how fast all of this was put together. It will be a miracle if it all goes well tomorrow. Please cross your fingers for me."

Margaret looked around the room. "We'll all be there. So we'll do more than just cross fingers. We'll be there to help with anything you need."

Everyone nodded in agreement.

Sarah took a relieved deep breath. "I can't thank you enough, guys."

Liz cut in, "Donna, tell us about the beach cleanup. You said there were hundreds of tires in the dunes?"

Donna shook her head. "Unreal, isn't it? It was discovered during one of the cleanup events. We had tons of volunteers come to clean them up and get them onto trucks for proper disposal, and we did it in one day. All of this has motivated

Dale and me to do more for the local environment and community, so we're discussing some fundraiser ideas for the future."

Dale nodded and stood up to clear some plates. "She's right. We're excited to help out where we can going forward." He paused to glance inside of the house. "By the way, anyone ready for dessert? Margaret brought brownies, and I've got ice cream."

As Dale and Donna began gathering dishes and bringing out dessert, the conversation shifted to lighter topics. Margaret found herself observing her friends with a sense of contentment. Despite challenges and anxieties, there was a solid foundation of support among them all.

Nick and Lisa sat close together at the table, occasionally showing each other something on Nick's phone, probably pictures of his new bay house. Greg and Liz were deep in animated conversation with Dave about their plans for the restored space. Donna was describing some city council drama to Chris, who listened with amused interest.

Sarah caught Margaret watching and moved to the empty chair beside her. "Thanks for the vote of confidence about tomorrow," she said quietly. "I'm probably overthinking it."

"That's what friends are for," Margaret replied. "And for what it's worth, I really do think you'll impress Blake Terry."

Sarah smiled, some of the tension leaving her shoulders. "How are you feeling about the beach house? Finding those letters must have been pretty special."

"It was," Margaret admitted. "There's something about uncovering pieces of William and Eleanor's story that feels important, like we're meant to know what happened to them. Today, we found more to the mystery—photographs of them hidden under a floorboard in an old box. The mystery deepens."

"That's exciting. Maybe you'll find the rest of their story as the renovation continues," Sarah suggested.

"I hope so," Margaret said.

CHAPTER ELEVEN

Sarah arrived at the Cape May Movie Theater three hours before Blake Terry was scheduled to appear. Her stomach had been in knots all day—a mixture of excitement, anxiety, and disbelief that this was actually happening.

"You're early," James said, greeting her at the stage door. He was dressed more formally than usual, in pressed slacks and a button-down shirt.

"I wanted to make sure everything was perfect," Sarah replied, clutching her clipboard with the evening's detailed itinerary. "Any issues I should know about?"

James shook his head. "We're right on schedule. The stage is set up exactly as requested—lectern, comfortable chair for the reading portion, and a small table for water. Sound check is complete. Blake's team will arrive about ninety minutes before doors open."

Sarah let out a breath. "Thanks for being so accommodating on such short notice."

"Are you kidding? This is the most exciting thing to happen here in a while," James said with a grin. "The phone's been ringing nonstop with people trying to get tickets."

"Same at the Book Nook," Sarah said. "I had to bring in extra help just to manage the calls."

They walked through the theater together, checking final details. The stage looked immaculate. It was intimate despite the size of the venue, with soft lighting focused on the center area where Blake would stand. Rows of chairs filled the orchestra level, and the balconies had been opened to accommodate the overflow. Three hundred twenty-seven seats in total, all sold within hours of the announcement.

"Sarah!" Margaret called from the lobby entrance. She was carrying a large box, with Liz right behind her, holding another. "Where do you want these?"

"What are those?" Sarah asked, hurrying over.

"Programs," Margaret explained. "Nothing fancy, just a single sheet with Blake's bio and book information. And the Book Nook's address prominent at the bottom, of course."

Sarah lifted one from the box. "These are beautiful. Let's put them on the tables in the lobby for now."

As they arranged the programs, the rest of their friends began to arrive. Dave and Greg carried in boxes of books from Sarah's store, setting them up on tables that had been placed in the theater's spacious lobby. Donna and Dale came with elegant flower arrangements for the stage and entrance. Nick and Lisa arrived with baskets of gift bags that contained the Book Nook bookmarks, Cape May postcards, and discount coupons for the store.

"Chris is setting up at the Book Nook," Sarah explained when Liz asked about his whereabouts. "Hobbling around in that walking boot of his, arranging the refreshments for the after-party. I told him to just come to the theater and relax in a seat, but he insisted on helping."

* * *

An hour before the doors were to open, a sleek black SUV pulled up to the rear entrance. James rushed to alert Sarah, who was giving last-minute instructions to the volunteers who would be ushering.

"She's here," he said in a stage whisper, his eyes wide with excitement.

Sarah smoothed her dress and took a deep breath. "Okay. Let's go greet her."

They walked to the back entrance together, where a small security team was already coordinating with the theater's staff. The vehicle door opened, and Blake Terry stepped out, followed by a woman Sarah assumed was her publicist and two assistants carrying leather bags.

Blake was taller in person than Sarah had expected, dressed in an elegant pantsuit that somehow looked both casual and sophisticated. Her famous smile was just as captivating off-screen, and when she extended her hand to Sarah, there was a genuine warmth in her eyes.

"You must be Sarah. I'm Blake. Thank you so much for arranging this."

Sarah shook her hand, trying to appear professional despite her inner fangirl screaming. "It's an honor to have you here, Blake. Welcome to Cape May."

Sarah introduced James, who led the group inside, giving a brief tour of the backstage area. Blake seemed genuinely impressed by the historic theater, pausing to admire the ornate details of the architecture. James then led Blake and her team to the green room.

At precisely seven p.m., the doors opened, and the crowd began to flow in. The atmosphere was electric—a buzz of excitement filling the historic theater as people found their seats. Many stopped to purchase books in advance, creating a steady line at the tables, where Dave, Greg, and Lisa were working.

By seven forty-five, the theater was completely full. Sarah

stood at the back, watching as the last few attendees were seated. Her heart was pounding with a mixture of pride and nervous anticipation. This was by far the biggest event she'd ever organized, and so far, everything was running smoothly.

At eight sharp, the house lights dimmed, and James walked onto the stage to welcome everyone. He spoke briefly about the theater's history and recent restoration before introducing Sarah.

Taking a deep breath, Sarah walked to the center of the stage. The spotlight was warmer than she'd expected, and for a moment, the sea of faces before her was intimidating. But then she spotted her friends in the third row, Margaret giving her a subtle thumbs-up, and her nerves settled.

"Good evening, everyone," she began, her voice steady despite her racing heart. "I'm Sarah, owner of the Book Nook. When Blake Terry's publicist contacted me about a possible book signing, I never imagined we'd be gathered here tonight in this magnificent venue. I want to thank James and his team at the Cape May Movie Theater for accommodating us on such short notice and my incredible friends who made this event possible in less than a week."

There was appreciative applause, and Sarah continued, "Tonight, we have the privilege of hearing from one of the most talented actresses of our generation. Her performances have moved us, inspired us, and sometimes challenged us. And now, she's sharing her story in her own words. Please join me in welcoming Academy Award winner and author Blake Terry."

The audience erupted in applause as Blake walked onto the stage, waving graciously.

"Thank you, Sarah, for that kind introduction," Blake began once the applause had died down. "And thank you all for coming out tonight. I'm truly honored to be here in Cape May, a town I've heard so much about but never had the chance to visit until now."

She paused, looking out at the audience with a smile that

reached her eyes. "Before I begin, I'd like to acknowledge the beauty of this historic theater. I understand that Katherine Duffield was instrumental in funding its restoration. Katherine and I worked together on a film years ago, and she was as remarkable off-screen as she was on. This theater is a testament to her generosity and her commitment to preserving cultural spaces."

From her position at the side of the stage, Sarah watched as Blake captivated the audience from her very first words. There was something magnetic about her presence—a quality that drew people in and made them lean forward in their seats, eager to catch every word.

"My journey to this stage—both literally and figuratively—has been anything but straightforward," Blake continued, moving away from the lectern to stand center stage. "Many of you know me from my films, perhaps from my Academy Award speech, or maybe just from those gossip magazines at the checkout counter."

This earned a ripple of laughter from the audience.

"But the path that led me here began long before the cameras were rolling. It began in a modest two-bedroom apartment in Chicago, where my parents juggled multiple jobs—my father as a factory worker and my mother waiting tables—to raise three children while stretching every dollar. In our household, dreams often took a backseat to practical needs, but my parents never let us believe they were entirely out of reach."

For the next hour, Blake shared her story with a candor that was both surprising and moving. She spoke of early rejections—hundreds of them—and the odd jobs she'd worked to pay the bills. She described the challenge of balancing motherhood with her career, sometimes having to bring her young daughter to auditions when childcare fell through.

"There were moments," she said, her voice softening, "when I was ready to give up. When the constant 'no' began to feel like a personal indictment rather than just part of the process. After a particularly difficult day of rejections, I came home and told my husband I was done."

She paused, looking out at the audience. "He listened patiently, let me cry it out, and then asked one simple question: 'If you quit now, will you regret it when you're eighty?' The answer was immediately clear. Of course I would. So I kept going, not because I was certain I'd succeed but because I knew I'd regret not trying."

There were nods of recognition throughout the audience. Many were discreetly wiping away tears.

Blake moved on to discuss her breakthrough role, which had come after fifteen years of working in the industry, and the complicated feelings that accompanied sudden success.

"People often talk about 'overnight success,'" she said with a wry smile. "But those of us who've lived it know there's no such thing. There are just years of hard work that others didn't see followed by a moment when they finally do."

She shared behind-the-scenes stories from some of her most famous films, including a few surprisingly candid anecdotes about difficult costars—without naming names—and on-set mishaps that had never made it to the press.

"The reality of filmmaking is far less glamorous than people imagine," she said with a laugh. "I've spent entire days lying in mud for a single shot, worn the same costume for weeks until it could practically stand on its own, and once had to film a romantic scene after my costar ate an onion sandwich for lunch."

The audience laughed, completely enthralled by this glimpse behind the Hollywood curtain.

As she neared the end of her talk, she looked out at the audience, her expression earnest. "We all have stories of resilience. We all face obstacles. Mine happen to have played out with cameras watching, but they're not so different from yours. And that's why I wanted to write this book—not to share celebrity gossip, though there's a bit of that too," she added with a playful smile. "But to remind us all that behind the glamour and the accolades, we're just people trying our best to navigate this complicated life."

Blake concluded by reading a moving passage from her memoir about the night of her Academy Award win and the bittersweet reality of celebrating without her father, who had passed away just months earlier.

When she finished reading, there was a moment of complete silence before the theater erupted in applause, the audience rising to their feet in a standing ovation that continued for several minutes.

Blake seemed genuinely moved by the response. She thanked the audience and then opened the floor for questions. For the next thirty minutes, she answered thoughtfully, sometimes humorously, and always with remarkable honesty. She spoke about upcoming projects, her writing process, and her advocacy work for various causes.

As the Q and A session came to a close, Blake thanked everyone again and reminded them of the book signing at the Book Nook. "I've heard it's a magical place," she said, "and I can't wait to see it and meet more of you there."

* * *

At the after party at the Book Nook, they found Chris had transformed the space. Soft jazz played in the background, the lighting was masterfully dimmed, and tables had been set up with elegant displays of hors d'oeuvres and wine. A signing table had been arranged in one of the rear corners, with Blake's memoir prominently displayed on a custom stand. Despite his walking boot, Chris was hobbling from table to table, making final adjustments to the displays.

"Chris, this looks amazing," Sarah said, taking it all in. "But you should be sitting down with that foot."

He waved off her concern with a smile. "It's fine. I've been managing."

They had barely finished setting up when the first guests began to arrive. Within twenty minutes, the store was filled to capacity, with a line stretching down the block.

Greg, Dave, and Nick quickly stepped in to help direct traffic, while Donna, Dale, and Lisa assisted with serving refreshments. Liz and Margaret worked the registers, processing the steady stream of book purchases.

The atmosphere was festive—a cocktail party buzz filled the air as people discussed Blake's talk, sharing their favorite moments and insights. The wine flowed freely, and the trays of hors d'oeuvres needed constant replenishing.

When Blake arrived, she was greeted with another round of applause. She took her place at the signing table, and the line began to move steadily as she personalized each book, taking time to chat briefly with every person.

Chris had positioned himself near the refreshment table, attempting to balance on his good foot while arranging wineglasses. "This is the busiest I've ever seen the Book Nook," he said to Sarah as they restocked the wine cooler. "The store will be sold out of everything by the end of the night."

"I'm already sold out of Blake's memoir," Sarah replied with a smile. "We're taking orders for a second shipment now."

The evening stretched on, the crowd thinning only slightly as the hours passed. By eleven o'clock, Blake had signed hundreds of books, and the line outside had finally disappeared.

As the last few customers made their purchases and said their goodbyes, Blake's team began packing up their belongings.

Blake approached Sarah, who was cleaning up behind the counter.

"Sarah," she said, her voice slightly hoarse from hours of talking, "I wanted to thank you personally before we leave.

This has been one of the most extraordinary stops on my book tour."

"Really?" Sarah couldn't hide her surprise. "But you've been to New York, Los Angeles, Chicago..."

Blake smiled. "Those were wonderful in their own way, but there's something special about tonight. The historic theater, this charming bookstore, the warmth of this community... it's reminded me why I love these smaller venues. There's a connection here that you don't get in the larger cities."

Sarah felt a swell of pride. "That means so much to hear. We were thrilled to host you."

"I wish I could stay longer and actually experience Cape May properly," Blake continued. "From the little I've seen, it seems like a remarkable place."

"You'll have to come back," Sarah suggested. "Maybe when you're not on a book tour and can actually relax."

"I'd love that," Blake replied, and her tone suggested she meant it. "Maybe next summer. I hear the beaches are spectacular."

"They are," Sarah confirmed. "And we have accommodations that would offer the privacy you'd need."

Blake's publicist approached, politely indicating it was time to leave. "Our car is waiting, Blake. We have an early flight tomorrow."

With final hugs and thank-yous, Blake and her team departed, leaving the Book Nook feeling suddenly quiet despite the handful of people still helping with cleanup.

Sarah's friends gathered around her as the door closed behind Blake.

"Well," Dave said, raising a glass of the remaining wine, "I'd say that was a smashing success."

"Absolutely," Margaret agreed. "Sarah, you should be incredibly proud."

Sarah looked around at her friends—all of whom had worked tirelessly to make the evening a success—and at her beloved bookstore, which had just hosted one of the most famous actresses in the world.

"I couldn't have done it without all of you," she said, her voice thick with emotion. "Truly."

Chris started to stand from his stool, wincing as he put weight on his booted foot.

"Don't you dare," Donna warned him. "We'll come to you."

"Group hug!" Liz declared, and they all crowded in around Chris, laughing and slightly giddy from the excitement of the evening.

As they broke apart, Sarah raised her own glass. "To friends who make the impossible possible. And to Blake Terry—may she actually return to Cape May when she's not on tour."

"To Blake," they echoed, clinking their glasses together.

CHAPTER TWELVE

Margaret stood in the small bedroom, applying a final coat of paint to the wall. The soft cream color brightened the space, transforming what had been a dingy, forgotten room into something fresh and inviting. Eleven days into their renovation project, and already, the beach house was beginning to feel like theirs.

From downstairs came the sound of Dave's phone ringing, followed by his voice answering. Margaret continued painting, her mind drifting to the photos she'd discovered just days earlier. The faces of William and Eleanor had brought their love story to life in a way the letters alone couldn't. She found herself wondering about them constantly now, about what had happened after that final photograph—their engagement in September 1955.

"Margaret!" Dave called up the stairs. "Phone for you!"

She set her paintbrush across the top of the paint can and wiped her hands on a rag before heading downstairs. Dave stood in the living room, holding his phone out to her.

"It's Howard," Dave explained. "He was checking in on how the renovations are going. I figured you'd like to talk to him," he said with a knowing wink.

Margaret took the phone, suddenly eager. "Howard! How are you?"

"Doing just fine, Margaret," Howard's warm voice came through the line. "Dave was telling me about the plumbing work and those built-in bookshelves he's putting in. Sounds like you two are making real progress."

"We are," Margaret said, wandering toward the window as she spoke. "It's a lot of work, but we're starting to see the potential. The house has such good bones."

"That, it does," Howard agreed. "Pat and I always knew we'd found something special when we bought it. Raised all our kids there, as you know."

Margaret hesitated then decided to ask the question that had been burning in her mind. "Howard, I hope you don't mind me asking, but we found some things in the house. Letters and photographs from previous owners named William and Eleanor. Did you ever hear anything about them?"

There was a pause on the line, and then Howard chuckled. "William and Eleanor Phillips? Well, I'll be. I haven't thought about them in years."

Margaret's heart quickened. "You knew them?"

"Oh yes," Howard said. "They stopped by a few years after Pat and I moved in. Must have been around 1970 or so. They wanted to see the house one last time before they moved to California. William had gotten some fancy new job out there."
"They were in their forties then, I'd say. Their youngest had just graduated high school and was heading off to college. They spent an afternoon with Pat and me, sitting on the porch, drinking tea, reminiscing about their years at the cottage. How special it was to them. How special Cape May was."

"Did they tell you why they sold the house?" Margaret asked, catching Dave's eye. He had moved closer, listening intently to her side of the conversation.

"They said they simply outgrew it," Howard explained. "They had four kids in that little house. Eventually moved more inland, where houses were cheaper and William's commute to Philadelphia was shorter. But that cottage—they spoke about it like it was magical. Like it held all their best memories."

"Four children," Margaret repeated softly. They had built a family together after all.

"They've both passed, not too long ago," Howard added. "Eleanor went first, and William followed shortly after, from what I understand. It's been a few years now."

"Thank you for telling me this," Margaret said, emotion welling in her throat. "We found their letters and photographs, and I've been wondering what happened to them."

"They were good people," Howard said. "They seemed as happy as can be when they visited—holding hands like newlyweds even after all those years. Pat always said we had big shoes to fill, keeping up the love that house had seen."

After a few more minutes of conversation about the renovations and promises to send photos of their progress, Margaret ended the call and turned to Dave.

"They lived long, happy lives together," she said, a smile spreading across her face. "Four children. They moved inland to be closer to Philadelphia eventually. They came back to visit the house years later, still in love."

Dave wrapped an arm around her shoulders. "That's wonderful. I'm glad their story had a happy ending."

Margaret's eyes suddenly widened. "Wait a minute." She hurried over to where her notepad lay on the kitchen counter. "There was something in Eleanor's diary. Something about William hiding things in the house…"

She flipped through her notes, scanning for the relevant passage. "Here it is! Eleanor mentioned William hiding tokens of their relationship throughout the house and property. One of them was 'secret messages on cellar stones written in invisible ink that could only be revealed when held to a flame.'"

"The stones?" Dave repeated, glancing toward the door that led to the cellar.

"We have to check," Margaret said, already moving toward the cellar door. "Do we have candles?"

Dave laughed. "I think there are some in that emergency kit in the car. But Margaret, you don't really think—"

"I absolutely think," she interrupted, her eyes bright with excitement. "Grab a flashlight too!"

Five minutes later, they stood in the damp basement, flashlight beams dancing across the old stone foundation walls. Dave had brought a small candle, which he lit and held carefully.

"What exactly are we looking for?" he asked.

"I'm not sure," Margaret admitted, running her fingers along the rough stones. "The diary mentioned messages written in invisible ink on the foundation stones. Maybe there's one that looks different somehow."

They moved slowly around the perimeter of the cellar, examining each stone. Most were solid, firmly set in place with old mortar, but as Margaret reached a section near one of the back corners, she noticed something unusual.

"Dave, look at this one," she called, pointing at a stone that appeared slightly different from those surrounding it. "The mortar around it looks newer or at least different."

Dave joined her, holding the flashlight closer. "You're right. And it's a slightly different color from the others."

Margaret's heart raced. "Can I have the candle?"

Dave handed it to her, and Margaret held the flame close to the stone, moving it slowly across the surface. At first, nothing happened, but then, as the heat of the flame warmed the stone, faint marks began to appear.

Margaret gasped. "Dave, look! There's something written here!"

As they watched, words appeared on the stone's surface,

written in what must have been lemon juice or some other organic substance that had long since dried invisible:

Forever yours, in this home that holds our hearts. Look behind for the beginning of our forever. —W

"Behind?" Dave murmured. "Behind the stone?"

Margaret handed the candle back to Dave and pressed her fingers against the edges of the stone. It moved slightly under her touch.

"It's loose," she said, excitement building in her voice. "Help me pull it out."

Together, they worked the stone free from its setting. As it came loose, Margaret aimed her flashlight into the space behind it. Instead of seeing the dirt she expected, the beam illuminated an opening off to the side—a space much larger than the missing stone would account for.

"There's something back there," she whispered, leaning closer. "A hollow or a room or something."

Dave leaned in as well, his expression shifting from skepticism to wonder. "You're right. It looks like there's a space behind the wall. But how is that possible? This is supposed to be the foundation."

Margaret directed her flashlight beam further into the opening, revealing cobwebs and dust but also what appeared to be man-made walls within.

"Dave," she said slowly, "I think there's a hidden room back there."

Dave straightened, rubbing the back of his neck. "Well, this section of wall was on my list to repair anyway. The inspector said there was some water damage and possible rot behind it." He gestured to the wooden framing that covered the foundation in this section. "We'd have to tear it out to fix it properly."

Margaret looked at him hopefully. "So we could..."

Dave grinned. "I'll get my tools."

Thirty minutes later, they had carefully removed a section of the damaged wall covering, revealing what had once been a room built into a natural alcove in the foundation. It was small, no more than six feet by six feet, but it was unmistakably a deliberate space.

Margaret gasped as her flashlight illuminated the contents: a small wooden desk covered in dust, a chair pushed neatly against it, and what appeared to be a stack of yellowed paper on the desktop. Cobwebs hung from the ceiling and draped across every surface, untouched for what must have been decades.

"I can't believe this," Dave murmured, stepping carefully into the space. "Someone built a room down here then at some point closed it off."

"William," Margaret said confidently. "This must be what Eleanor meant in her diary—a secret place."

She approached the desk, her flashlight revealing more details. There was an old oil lamp, and beside it sat a small wooden box, ornately carved.

With trembling fingers, Margaret opened the box. Inside, nestled on a faded velvet lining, lay a silver key and a small porcelain bluebird, its blue glaze still vibrant despite the years.

"The tokens from the treasure hunt," she whispered. "The silver key and the bluebird that Eleanor mentioned in her diary."

Dave pulled the desk drawer open carefully, revealing more papers inside—envelopes similar to those they'd found in the shoebox upstairs, but these appeared to span a much longer time period. Some looked relatively newer, the paper less yellowed.

Margaret picked up one of the envelopes from the desk surface, noting the date: March 1957. She opened it carefully and read:

My dearest William,

As your business trip enters its third week, I find myself returning to this secret place you created for us. The children are asleep upstairs, unaware that their mother slips down to the basement each night to write to their father, even when their father is hundreds of miles away.

Little Thomas took his first steps yesterday, toddling across the kitchen floor with determination in his eyes—so like his father. Elizabeth asked when you'd be home to read her favorite story. "Only Daddy does the voices right," she insists. I promised it would be soon, though the days feel long without you.

The garden is beginning to show signs of spring. The roses you planted last fall have survived the winter and are beginning to bud. I've been thinking about expanding the vegetable garden this year—perhaps you can help design it when you return.

Until then, I leave this letter in our secret place, adding to the collection that chronicles our love. When you return, you'll find it waiting along with my heart.

Forever yours, Eleanor

Tears welled in Margaret's eyes as she finished reading. "They didn't stop writing to each other," she said softly. "Even after they were married, even after they had children. They kept writing these letters."

Dave picked up another envelope, this one dated 1963. "Listen to this one: 'My beloved Eleanor, as I sit in this hotel room in Chicago, missing the sound of your voice and the warmth of your presence, I find myself thinking of our secret room. How many letters have we exchanged over the years, tucked away in that private space where only we know to look? A decade of our hearts poured onto paper...'"

Margaret opened another drawer in the desk, revealing dozens more letters neatly bundled with string and labeled by year. The collection spanned from 1956 to 1969—thirteen years of correspondence, even though they were married and living in the same house for most of that time.

"They created their own private world," Margaret said, carefully replacing the letter she'd read. "A place where they could leave pieces of themselves for only each other to find."

Dave looked around the small room with new appreciation.

"And it stayed hidden all these years. Howard and Pat never found it."

"Maybe they didn't need to," Margaret suggested. "Perhaps they had their own special places, their own ways of keeping their love alive through the years."

They spent the next hour carefully examining the contents of the small room. Besides the letters, they found small gifts William and Eleanor had left for each other—a pressed flower, a smooth stone from the beach, a tiny sketch of the cottage drawn in William's hand. Each item told part of their story. Each letter revealed more about their life together.

* * *

As the day began winding down, Margaret and Dave strolled down Congress Street, taking a well-deserved break from their renovation work.

"I can't believe we've only been working on the house for eleven days," Margaret said, her hand comfortably nestled in Dave's. "It feels like we've been a part of its story much longer."

"That's because we have," Dave replied. "From the moment Howard told us about it, I think we knew it was meant to be ours."

They turned onto Jackson Street, where massive Victorian homes displayed their fall finery. Bright-orange and -yellow mums adorned porches, while tasteful Halloween decorations hinted at the upcoming holiday. The maple trees that lined the street had begun their autumn transformation, their leaves turning brilliant shades of red and gold.

"Look at that one," Margaret said, pointing to a particularly grand Victorian with an elaborate wraparound porch. "Can you imagine the stories it could tell?"

"Probably not as good as ours," Dave said with a smile. "Not every house has secret rooms and hidden love letters."

Margaret laughed, leaning into his side as they walked. "True. We lucked out on the romance-novel scale of house purchases."

They continued their leisurely exploration, venturing into residential areas Margaret hadn't fully explored despite her familiarity with the area. This was a different Cape May—not the bustling tourist area near the beach but the quieter neighborhoods where locals lived year-round.

"It's funny," Margaret said as they paused to admire a garden still vibrant with fall blooms. "I've spent so much time here over the years, but there are still streets I've never walked down, houses I've never noticed."

"That's the beauty of it," Dave replied. "There's always something new to discover, even in a place you think you know well."

A gentle breeze carried the distant sound of waves and the scent of salt as they made their way toward the Washington Street Mall. The shops were less crowded now that the summer season had ended, allowing them to stroll at a relaxed pace.

"Do you think William and Eleanor walked these same streets?" Margaret asked. "Shopped in these same stores?"

"Some of them, probably," Dave said. "The historic ones, anyway."

Margaret smiled at the thought. "I keep picturing them now—not just as the young couple from the photographs but as the family they became too. Four children running ahead of them down the beach, William and Eleanor following hand in hand."

They reached a small park and settled onto a bench. The late-afternoon light turned everything golden, casting a magical glow over the Victorian rooftops visible above the trees.

"When I think about it," Margaret continued, "that's what makes Cape May so special. It's not just about the beautiful architecture or the beaches. It's about the dreams that people bring here and build here generation after generation."

"Cape May dreams," Dave murmured, squeezing her hand. "First William and Eleanor's then Howard and Pat's and now ours."

"And someday, Harper and Abby might bring their families here," Margaret added. "Continue the tradition."

They sat in comfortable silence for a moment, watching as the sun dipped lower, painting the sky in deepening shades of orange and pink.

"We should head back," Dave said eventually. "I want to finish that piece of trim work before dinner."

Margaret nodded, but neither of them moved immediately. There was something perfect about this moment, something worth savoring.

"You know," she said finally, "when I first saw the beach house, I thought we were crazy to take on another renovation project. But now I can't imagine not having found it, not having discovered William and Eleanor's story."

"It was meant to be," Dave said simply. "Just like us."

As they walked back toward their beach house, Margaret felt a profound sense of connection—not just to Dave and their girls but to all those who had loved this special place before them as well. William and Eleanor, who had built their dream in the little cottage by the sea. Howard and Pat, who had filled it with the laughter of their own children. And now Margaret and Dave, continuing the legacy, weaving their own dreams into the fabric of Cape May.

The house was waiting for them when they returned, its windows catching the last golden light of day. It wasn't just a renovation project anymore. It was their Cape May dream, a dream shared across generations, a dream that would continue long after they were gone.

And somehow, Margaret thought as Dave opened the front door, that made it all the more precious.

EPILOGUE

The crackling fireplace filled the beach house living room with warmth as the November wind whistled outside the windows. Margaret stood in the doorway between the living room and the kitchen, a mug of tea warming her hands as she took in the transformation. What had been a well-loved but dated space just months ago now shone with fresh updates and thoughtful touches.

Dave adjusted one of the throw pillows on the new sectional sofa they'd chosen specifically for the space. The soft gray fabric complemented the cream walls and navy-blue accents throughout the room. The built-in bookshelves he'd crafted on either side of the fireplace were filled with books, sea glass they'd collected from the beach, and carefully chosen decorative items.

"It's perfect," Margaret said softly.

Dave looked up, a smile spreading across his face. "Worth every splinter and paint spill."

The kitchen gleamed with new stainless steel appliances, which contrasted beautifully with the refinished mahogany cabinets. The worn countertops had been replaced with a speckled quartz that reminded Margaret of sand. A small table sat in the corner by the windows, optimal for family breakfasts.

On the wall near the staircase hung a collection of black-and-white photographs in simple frames. Among them were two special additions: William and Eleanor standing together on the front porch, arms around each other, faces illuminated with joy; and Eleanor in the garden, kneeling beside her roses. Their smiles reached across time, connecting then to now in a tangible way.

The ceramic bluebird, carefully cleaned and polished by Margaret until its blue glaze gleamed, sat on the mantel above the fireplace. Beside it lay the silver key, both items displayed like the treasures they were.

"I can't believe how quickly it all came together," Dave said, joining Margaret by the doorway. "Remember how the kitchen looked when we first saw it?"

Margaret laughed. "How could I forget? That avocado-green tile in the bathroom was something else too."

"Now replaced with the subway tile of your dreams," Dave replied, wrapping an arm around her shoulders.

Margaret leaned into him, savoring the moment. The renovations had been exhausting but exhilarating. Weekends spent driving back and forth from their main home, late nights painting and assembling furniture, early mornings troubleshooting unexpected challenges. But now their vision had become reality: a cozy second home just blocks from the beach, a retreat they could escape to whenever the ocean called.

"I was thinking," Dave said, his voice tentative in the way it always was when he was about to suggest something he wasn't sure she'd like. "What would you think about spending Christmas here?"

Margaret turned to look at him, surprise evident on her face. "Christmas? Here?"

"Yeah," Dave continued, more confident now. "The girls would love it. We could decorate that corner with a real tree.

The fireplace works great now with the new flue and would keep us cozy. It would be something different."

As Margaret considered the idea, images began to form in her mind. The beach house dressed in evergreen garlands and twinkling lights. A Christmas tree adorned with ornaments, perhaps some new ones they could buy from one of the shops on the Washington Street Mall. Stockings hung from the mantel alongside the bluebird and key.

"We could walk on the beach Christmas morning," she said slowly, the idea taking root. "Bundle up against the cold and then come back to a warm fire."

Dave's eyes lit up. "Exactly. And we could cook our Christmas dinner in that new double oven. Maybe a ham?"

Margaret nodded, her excitement growing. "The girls could help decorate. We could start some new traditions."

"So that's a yes?" Dave asked, hopeful.

"It's definitely a yes," Margaret confirmed.

Dave hugged her close, and they stood together for a moment, imagining the holiday that waited just around the corner.

Outside, the first few Christmas lights had already appeared on neighboring houses, though Thanksgiving was still weeks away. The Victorian homes that lined the streets would soon be transformed with elegant holiday decorations, their historic charm enhanced by wreaths and garlands.

As the sun dipped below the horizon, Margaret's mind danced with possibilities. Lazy morning coffees by the tree. Evening walks to admire the decorated homes throughout Cape May. Perhaps some holiday shopping on the Washington Street Mall, where the shops would be dressed in their seasonal best. So many new memories waiting to be made.

"We should head back," Dave said eventually, glancing at his watch. "We told the girls we'd be home for dinner."

Margaret nodded reluctantly. "One more thing before we go."

She crossed to the built-in shelf and picked up the small notebook she'd left there earlier. It was new, its leather cover still stiff. On the first page, she'd written a single line: "The Beach House Diaries."

"What's that?" Dave asked, curious.

"I thought I'd start my own diary," Margaret explained. "A record of our time here, just like Eleanor kept. Something for future generations to find someday."

Dave smiled, understanding completely. "Our own chapter in the house's story."

* * *

Pick up book 17 in the Cape May Series**, Cape May Snowflakes,** to follow Margaret, Liz, Dave, and the rest of the bunch. This will be the second Cape May Christmas book.

Start book 1 in my new Ocean City series, **A Summer in Ocean City.**

ABOUT THE AUTHOR

Claudia Vance is a writer of women's fiction and clean romance. She writes feel good reads that take you to places you'd like to visit with characters you'd want to get to know.

She lives with her boyfriend and two cats in a charming small town in New Jersey, not too far from the beautiful beach town of Cape May. She worked behind the scenes on television shows and film sets for many years, and she's an avid gardener and nature lover.

Copyright © 2025 by Claudia Vance

All rights reserved.

No part of this book may be reproduced in any form or by any electronic or mechanical means, including information storage and retrieval systems, without written permission from the author, except for the use of brief quotations in a book review.

This is a work of fiction. Names, places, events, organizations, characters, and businesses are used in a fictitious manner or the product of the author's imagination.

Made in United States
North Haven, CT
20 July 2025